# THE JANUS GATE

## PAST PROLOGUE

# STAR TREK®
## THE ORIGINAL SERIES

book three of three

## THE JANUS GATE

# PAST PROLOGUE

L. A. Graf

Based upon STAR TREK®
created by Gene Roddenberry

POCKET BOOKS
New York London Toronto Sydney Singapore

An *Original* Publication of POCKET BOOKS

POCKET BOOKS, a division of Simon & Schuster, Inc.
1230 Avenue of the Americas, New York, NY 10020



This book is published by Pocket Books, a division of Simon & Schuster, Inc., under exclusive license from Paramount Pictures.



ISBN: 0-7434-4596-1

First Pocket Books printing July 2002

10 9 8 7 6 5 4 3 2 1



Printed in the U.S.A.

# THE JANUS GATE

## PAST PROLOGUE

# Chapter One

COLD BIT AT Kirk's cheeks as he followed his youngest crewman deeper into the frozen dark. The glow of the boy's carbide lamp barely disturbed the surface of the blackness, and it didn't soften the hard angles of the fresh ice sheets surrounding them at all. It only pushed the dark ahead of them, one cautious step at a time. Chekov followed the invisible line sketched for him by his compass and Kirk tried not to make the ensign any more nervous than he already was by treading on his heels as he followed.

The maps were good, Kirk thought, flipping through the painstakingly drawn pages and mentally reliving the landing party's passage through each of those chambers and tunnels as he did so. Amazingly good, considering they'd had to be re-created in the midst of everything else the group had gone through to get this far. Now they were close to being out of this subterranean icebox. The exit was only a few tens of meters over their heads—hot showers, full meals, and clean, dry uniforms were just a short vertical climb in their futures, and Kirk was as glad as anyone else to be done with this part of their adventure. At least he could attack the mystery of the starships scattered across Tlaoli's surface from the relative safety of his own bridge, with his crew safe and whole alongside him.

An unexpected bark, popping against the unseen walls of the cavern, yanked Kirk to a halt. He shot a quick look in the direction where the clatter seemed to settle, but, strain as he might, could only see the same opaque blackness that had hidden every other danger since they'd set foot in this cave. Kirk grabbed at Chekov's shoulder to halt him. "Do you hear that?" he asked urgently, releasing the boy to turn and check the party members they'd left near the entrance.

Heat from a sudden fire swarmed up into his face and knocked him to the ground.

Kirk's first instinct was to guard the map—the precious, re-created map that was their best insurance against wandering through these caves forever. He tucked it flat to the belly of his cave jumper and rolled facedown in the frozen mud to shield it from the flames. But just that quickly, the heat and light receded as though sucked out through a blasted airlock, and the ground beneath him was dry and hard and anomalously warm against his frost-reddened cheek.

He reached out one hand to slap at the ground in front of his face. Concrete. He'd fallen down in a cave on the fringes of the frontier, but he'd somehow landed on an expanse of what was unmistakably poured concrete.

Voices and sirens pushed Kirk's senses past what had been the unseen walls of the cavern, opening up the darkness into an expansive night with five tiny, bloody moons strung diagonally above the tree horizon like a necklace of badly set garnets. Dry leaves skated across the road in fits and starts, leaping spastically into the air where they were startled by hot thermals, then flashing into ash in the dragon's breath of flaming trees and burning buildings. Kirk heard someone cry out in a barking language that he knew wasn't human, but when he rolled to place the sound there was nothing to see but a still unburnt tree line dancing freakishly in the shadows from the fires across the way.

The staccato popping of antique firearms drew his stomach up into his throat even before the more familiar whine of phaser fire sang out in reply. *Starfleet.* Whatever was happening here, there were Starfleet people involved in it—maybe even his own people. He wasn't going to lie here on the ground and just wait for the battle to find him, not if there was anything he could do to help.

Stuffing the map down the front of his jumper, he scrambled to his feet and turned a circle to give himself a starting point from which to get his bearings. The road on which he stood was unlined and empty—like a logging road that went only one place and didn't need to supply any additional directions to what little traffic used it. An impressive deciduous forest walled one side, it's tattered canopy still scattering the dying leaves of early autumn. Across the road from the forest, a handful of older trees had been left to decorate the edges of a concrete-and-glass city that grew gradually taller as the buildings moved away from the road. It was on this side of the landscape that the fires burned.

Kirk stared toward the stair-step pyramids and cylindrical towers already swathed in robes of flame, until they stood out both bright and dark against the nighttime sky. *I should know this place.* Bits and pieces of memory jostled for attention at the back of his brain, only to be beaten into silence by the horrific scene in front of him. If he knew this town, this planet, it was in some vastly different context. Like a familiar painting, inexpertly recreated from a new and confusing angle. Or tourist streets seen at night when he'd previously only walked them during the day.

That he should know this place seemed terribly important—enough to make his heart pound faintly, like a drum still muffled by distance—but the front of his mind insisted, *No! Go find the others!* before he could spend too long trying to excavate the memory. Blinking hard, Kirk pulled his eyes away from the conflagration, and ducked into the cover of the tree line.

The road arced back toward the heart of the burning city, and the old growth forest followed it only partway. Kirk paused at the edge of the trees and crouched behind a massive trunk to survey the firelit expanse between forest and town. The road itself remained clear, but quick figures darted between buildings and immobile vehicles just inside the edges of the city. Some of them clumped together in terrified, stumbling groups as they scrambled toward perceived safety; others carried what were obviously weapons, although who or what they pursued wasn't always so clear.

Kirk fingered the collar of his gold cave jumper. Movement had cracked off the sheets of mud made brittle by the dry autumn air, leaving him pale and exposed. While his gold command tunic was only marginally darker, at least he had on black trousers and boots beneath the jumper, which would cut his visibility in half. Besides, he had a feeling that the moisture-wicking nano-weave was going to be about the least useful thing he could have brought here with him. He would much rather have had one of Martine's phasers, or at least one of Sanner's climbing ropes.

He stowed the folded jumper in a hollow beneath the tree's hunched up roots, burying it under a few large handfuls of leaf litter and hoping he'd be able to find the spot later if he needed it. He buried Chekov's notebook with its maps and attached mechanical pencil along with the jumper. He couldn't imagine what use he could possibly find for it, but it still somehow seemed ungrateful to just abandon it after forcing the boy to sit on the floor of a frozen cave and re-create the thing from memory.

The weapons fire had thinned, with only a single phaser wailing in futile response to increasingly bold chatters of gunfire. Kirk threaded between shrubbery and buildings, hugging walls as closely as he could so as to present the smallest possible target to anyone trying to shoot down on him from above. *It would help to know who's doing the shooting.* It would tell him what sort of tactics to expect, not to mention what sort of weapons and what sort of physical capabilities. He didn't like not knowing who the bad guys were.

As if in answer to his thoughts, a pair of gunmen clattered down the long flight of open-rail steps that wrapped around the building in front of Kirk. The metallic thunder of their footsteps rang hollowly somewhere in the back of Kirk's memory, and he suddenly knew the building at his shoulder was a tall extended-family dwelling without understanding how he knew that or why it should make the inside of his mouth taste like bile. When the first man to reach the ground lifted his head at the foot of the stairs, he looked across the neatly trimmed hedgerow and locked eyes with Kirk as though he'd known all along the captain would be there. And even his pale copper-penny eyes looked terrifyingly familiar to Kirk.

Kirk struck out before the man could swing his long weapon into firing position. Twisting to one side, Kirk jammed the muzzle of the rifle down toward the ground and landed a solid blow on the man's jaw without interrupting his turn. The momentum alone snapped the man's head aside and wrenched the rifle from his grasp. Still gripping the muzzle, Kirk stepped neatly over the toppled body and let the rifle's heavy metal stock finish its swing into the shins of the man above him on the stairs. A hissing thread of heat tore past very close to Kirk's skull, then the second man was down atop his partner, and Kirk had knocked him senseless with the butt of the first man's gun. He rubbed at his temple where the shot had narrowly missed him, and stared down at the unconscious bodies. He knew where he was now. He knew *when* he was. He just didn't understand how he had gotten here.

They were both obviously Grexxen—their faces a bronze so extreme it bordered on greenish, and their hair the same faded copper as their eyes. A little hair dye and a pair of dark glasses, and either of them could have passed as human in any metropolitan center on Earth. But they weren't human—they were Vragax. Even after all these years, thinking about that militant tribe of Grexxen natives filled Kirk's stomach with acid and made him want to spit out every foul epithet he'd ever heard. Because even after nineteen years he couldn't forget the helmetlike fall of Vragax braids, or the smell of their *puhen* oil-based warpaints, or the way they laughed at how humans died when they shot them down in the streets.

He shook both men out of their pants with no more care than he'd have shown a sack full of potatoes. Tying them both to the stairs, he took their weapons and every power cell and munition they had between them. One of them also had a string of handheld explosives. The other had a radio that didn't appear to be picking anything up on its open frequency. Kirk turned it off to keep it silent, then threw it as far away into the bushes as he could.

The streets were familiar now. Eerily undersized, as though he'd expanded them in his memory, and still uncomfortable in that tourist-streets-after-dark way. He remembered abruptly that his father had never let them leave the embassy grounds after nightfall. "It's not a curfew," George Kirk had insisted. "I just won't have any boys of mine showing disrespect for the local authorities with their shenanigans." As though the shenanigans of two human boys could have inspired anything to rival what had finally gone down on this planet.

He checked both the charges and the loads on the gauss rifles as he jogged, almost by memory, back toward the burning Starfleet embassy. They both had several hours' use still in them, and more than sixty shots between them, not counting reloads. He flipped the switch to single shot to save on ammunition. Unlike the Vragax, he had no use for mowing down large swaths of the civilian population with every squeeze of the trigger. Anything he couldn't do one bullet at a time, he wasn't interested in doing at all.

He found the shuttle nose-down in the lawn of a Kozhu-run infant-care facility, half-buried in the dirt it had ploughed up ahead of its long skid, like a dead giant beneath a carelessly thrown shroud. Just like he remembered it. It was easier to see what had killed it, now that he was older and understood better what to look for. A small, exhaust-seeking microbolt had blown away the rear of one nacelle and part of the stern bulkhead. The remaining engine had been just enough to let Ensign Leone put them down in something more like a landing than a crash, but not enough to let either Zeke Leone or his copilot walk away from the attempt. The shuttle had split open on impact, trailing debris and bodies behind it for a hundred meters. The fact that neither the Vragax nor the Kozhu were supposed to have surface-to-air weaponry powerful enough to take down a Starfleet shuttle hadn't saved Leone or the other men who'd gone down on the shuttle with him.

Kirk ducked behind the mound of steaming dirt, just beside where the shattered pilot's seat should have been. Across the shuttle's nose from him, nine men in the red-and-black of Starfleet security littered the torn-up ground like broken dolls. Kirk closed his eyes against the memory of their leader seizing him by the front of his shirt and commanding, *"Go! Get back to the embassy and tell your dad we need backup!"* And, God help him, Kirk had gone. He'd wriggled out the back of the dying shuttle and left them, telling himself it was an order, telling himself he was doing the right thing and that his father would bring back a combat team that would know exactly what to do.

But as fast as he ran, as hard as he tried, he never saw the embassy or Lieutenant Maione's squad again. Until now.

Grabbing the lip of the shuttle's buckled roof, Kirk pulled himself up and over, careful to roll down the other side as swiftly as possible and drop into a crouch in the deep shadows there. He couldn't tell how long it had been since the Vragax natives had finished their slaughter here, but he didn't want to risk being targeted by whoever might still be lurking in the burning darkness that used to be Sogo city. The men around him had been killed by whatever the Vragax had on hand—magnetic propulsion gauss slugs, phasers, the short ceremonial darts from Vragax spear throwers. Kirk knew Maione's men must have taken down a good many Vragax with them, but there were no native bodies mixed in with the carnage. In the midst of their bloody rampage through Sogo, the Vragax still took time to collect their own dead for whatever it was they considered dignified disposal.

Kirk sensed more than saw a furtive movement toward the rear of the shuttle, dark-on-dark, almost silent despite the bits of broken shuttle and restless autumn leaves. Sinking back against the rucked-up earth, Kirk thumbed the primer on one of the gauss rifles and lifted it slowly to his shoulder. The chain of tiny electromagnets lining the inside of its barrel whined almost beyond the pitch of human hearing as they built up the necessary charge.

The shadow creeping up on Kirk along the shuttle's splintered flank halted. "John?" Tension poised the burly silhouette so still it might have been a statue. "Maione, is that you?"

It could have been a recording of Kirk's own voice. *Why did I never notice that before?* he wondered. Swallowing hard, he let the gauss rifle sink to rest across his knees. "Maione's dead." He hoped he sounded confident and in control. He hoped he didn't sound too much like himself. "I'm the only one left."

The other human padded closer, hunkering down on all fours to share Kirk's shadow and the relative protection of the artificial hill. There wasn't enough light to really see him clearly, but Kirk knew even through the darkness that his uniform was Starfleet, his tunic red, and his eyes were the same angry green as the East Coast ocean in winter. He was a commander, he was forty-six years old, and he was the meanest son of a bitch to ever head a security squad. "Name and rank," the man snapped, reaching for the second gauss rifle without asking, much less waiting, for position.

"Forester." Kirk blurted the name without thinking, then was forced to add, "Captain," because he wouldn't be able to hide the braid on his sleeves. "I came in with the last group of replacements."

The other man nodded as though he'd expected as much. "I didn't even get a chance to read you in, sir. My apologies."

Kirk felt an oddly uncomfortable blush push up into his face. "None necessary." *Because I wasn't really here—I shouldn't be here now—* But he made himself ask steadily, "What's your name, soldier?" as though the answer would hardly make any difference, as though he didn't already know.

"Commander George Kirk, sir, interim security chief." He powered up his rifle, then helped himself to one of Kirk's spare clips and shoved it into the half-empty magazine. "And I'm out here, sir, because I'm looking for my son."

For the second time in twenty-four hours, Uhura found herself standing shocked and helpless in the blue glow of Tlaoli's Janus Gate. The first time she had felt this paralyzing fear was when Captain Kirk and Ensign Chekov had disappeared without warning as they tried to evacuate a trapped caving team from these ice-sheathed caverns. Now, with the alien time transporter they had discovered here free of its distorting travertine shell and obediently responding to Spock's commands, the source of her shock was a phalanx of metal-clad aliens who had just banned them from ever using the Janus Gate again.

With all her heart, Uhura wished the time transporter would whip out a glowing blue curtain and make these enigmatic intruders disappear, the same way it had taken their missing captain. But the Janus Gate's power stores were once again exhausted, and the fiery glow at its heart had shrunk back down to a sapphire flicker. Despite the drizzle and mist from the ice melting all around them, Uhura could see that the armored bodies of the cybernetic aliens had linked together to form a solid metal stockade around the Gate.

The aliens who called themselves Shechenag had descended as silently as spiders, gliding down frictionless wires from the solution pits in the ceiling. They had timed their entrance perfectly—the unwary moment when triumph and relief had swept through the *Enterprise* crewmen after they successfully used the Janus Gate to haul Lieutenant Sulu back from the distant future to which he'd been sent. The tense and exhausting hour Uhura had spent as the focus of the alien device had been worth it: Her quest across time had brought back not only their missing helmsman but also the future version of Chekov who'd helped Sulu survive a hellish future where the Gorn ruled the galaxy.

But there had been no time to celebrate. Before they could use the Janus Gate to try to rescue Captain Kirk from his own past, before Sulu and Chekov had even been retrieved from the healing chamber where the Janus Gate had sent them, a horde of metallic insects had plunged down into their midst, using metallic claws with stinging electrical anodes to herd them all to the edge of the cavern. Any attempt to resist—or even to retain their equipment, as archaeologist Carolyn Palamas had tried to do with her visual translating device—had been met with such swift and ruthless punishment that the victims were either still shaking with residual shock or, like Security Guard Yuki Smith, completely unconscious.

"How is she, Doctor?" Spock asked McCoy quietly while the Shechenag clicked and whistled among themselves, apparently consulting each other on their next move. It was very odd to see the glittering translucent bodies of the actual aliens inside the clear shells of their armored suits, turning back and forth toward one another as the conversation rattled among them.

"I think she's just been knocked unconscious." McCoy looked up from the sprawled body of the security guard, putting his old-fashioned stethoscope back into the chest pocket of his caving suit. The anxious faces of young Ensign Chekov and an even younger James T. Kirk craned past the shoulders of the other members of the party to listen to the doctor's verdict. "If she doesn't wake up pretty soon, though, it might mean something more serious is wrong."

"This one of your species is not injured." The flat machine-generated tone of that voice would have told Uhura it came from among the line of Shechenag even if she hadn't seen Spock turn his head and lift one eyebrow at the speaker. Inside the perfectly still metallic casing, several spindly limbs gesticulated for emphasis. "This one received only mild electron overdose to suppress aggressive behavior."

"Are her symptoms consistent with electrical shock, Doctor?" the Vulcan science officer asked.

McCoy lifted one of Smith's eyelids. "Yes. They're also consistent with giving herself a concussion when she hit the ground." He lowered his voice to a grumble. "Spock, I don't like the idea that those walking tin cans over there are listening to everything we say."

"Indeed," said the Vulcan. "However, lowering your voice is not a logical response to the situation, Doctor. I believe it is safe to assume that their sound detectors are equally as advanced as the rest of their technology."

Uhura wrenched her gaze away from the aliens barricading the Janus Gate, although part of her still desperately wanted to watch to make sure no other insectoid robots detached themselves from those odd metallic bodies. "Mr. Spock, they learned our language from the archaeological translator," she said, in flawless Vulcan. "But it was only programmed for an English translation."

The science officer's slanted eyebrows went up again, this time in appreciation. "A fact which I should have remembered, Lieutenant," he replied in the same language. "Especially since I distinctly recall noting its ethnocentricity in naming the transporter for the human god Janus rather than the Vulcan goddess Yelanna." Spock eyed the Shechenag watching them, then switched abruptly to Andorian. "By using no more than a dozen phonemes from any one language, we should be able to confuse any translating device they might have brought with them."

Uhura glanced at the blank faces around them. "As well as most of our crewmates," she reminded Spock in Andorian, then deliberately turned her back on the

Shechenag and gave the rest of their team the Starfleet hand signal that meant, *Covert communication only, enemy is listening.*

What felt like a sharp metallic caliper closed on Uhura's shoulder, tight enough to startle a gasp out of her. There was a flash of black and violet motion between the other bodies, and she suddenly found herself standing between the older versions of both Chekov and Sulu, both of them clearly poised to attack if the Shechenag did anything more threatening. With a hiss of sophisticated gears and tiny bearings, however, the alien merely rotated its limb to bring Uhura around to face it, then released her.

"This one will face us so we can see all of its attachments," the alien said, with no more emphasis or emotion in its voice than before. Inside its clear shell, however, two small stalked eyes swiveled in what looked almost like a glare. "Operations intended to reactivate this device will not be permitted. You have ten hours to leave this system. Departure from this cave should be immediate."

"That sound definite," McCoy said in halting schoolboy French. "We leave?"

Uhura had to bite her lip against a hysterical giggle, since the expression on Spock's lean face would have done credit to the most chauvinistic Frenchman. "We intend to leave," he said in English, answering both the doctor and the alien facing them. "An immediate departure, however, will require a transporter beam to be generated from our ship. With your permission, I will contact them—"

Uhura tried to school her face to look perfectly calm, but she felt her heart leap with excitement as she recognized Spock's ingenious strategy. If the Shechenag didn't know that the transporter beam would repower the Janus Gate rather than take them back to the *Enterprise,* there was a chance they could get the hostile aliens trapped in one of the random subspace warps that floated around the alien device when it was fully charged.

After a moment's pause, however, a burst of chattering from the other Shechenag made the one closest to them step back. A flush of colors passed across the surface of its floating chitinous body, although Uhura couldn't be sure if that represented a flush of strong emotion or just a rapid mental reassessment of the situation. Inside the clear torso tank, its stalked eyes elevated to peer at Spock with what looked like sudden attentiveness.

"Operations intended to reactivate this device will not be permitted." There wasn't the slightest variation in the Shechenag's machine-generated voice, but two of its clawlike appendages flashed upward with violent swiftness. Uhura was abruptly shouldered backward between the older versions of Chekov and Sulu, and had to stand on tiptoe to peer over their shoulders. The cybernetic alien had made no other move toward them. Inside its clear tank, the small floating body was also pointing upward, making it clear that its motion was intended to be directional. "Immediate evacuation can also occur using these ropes," it said. "No disabling has been done to your shuttlecraft. One trip back to your ship will be permitted."

Uhura saw the older version of Sulu glance over his shoulder at his younger counterpart. "Will the shuttle carry all of us in one trip?" he asked in fluent Japanese.

"If we throw out everything including the bulkhead supplies?" the younger pilot replied in the same language. "Maybe."

The older Sulu glanced at the man standing beside him, with the odd bittersweet smile Uhura had seen him use when his sense of amusement was tickled by something other people might think morbid. "We're expendable now, Pavel," Sulu said in rough but understandable Russian. "You want to stay down here and see if we can peel some of these shrimp out of their shells?"

"That may not forward our goals, Captain," Spock informed him in much better Russian, before Chekov could answer. Uhura wasn't sure how the Vulcan managed it, but his voice sounded equally formal and mannered in every language he used. "And there is a distinct probability that you will be needed more for later actions." He switched back to English, turning to meet the translucent gaze of the Shechenag who had issued the evacuation orders. "We will depart in the shuttle when we have transported all members of our party to it. However, we may not be able to leave the system within ten hours, because of the disabled status of our warp engines."

"You are given ten hours to depart the system." Perhaps because of its lack of anything like human emotion, the mechanical voice sounded completely implacable to Uhura. "If you are still within the system after ten hours, you will not be able to depart."

"Are you threatening to attack us?" Spock inquired politely.

The alien's metallic body took an odd, swaying step backward on its multiply jointed legs. "We are Shechenag," it said, just as it had done when it first spoke to them. There was a pause, as if that should have been enough explanation for them. When Spock continued to meet its gaze inquiringly, the alien rattled off something in its native tongue and was answered by a clattering chorus from its comrades. "Shechenag once made war for nine millennia," said the toneless voice. "We make no war now. After ten hours, nothing departs or enters this system for one thousand years. You are warned."

Spock surprised Uhura with a polite inclination of his head toward their captors. "We thank you for the warning," he said, then glanced over his shoulder. In the back of the group, the younger Chekov and Kirk were helping a groaning Yuki Smith to her feet. "Mr. Sanner, please climb up to the cave entrance above us so that we may begin evacuating everyone."

"Spock, you *coq au vin!*" Even in his atrocious

French, McCoy's voice sounded recognizably indignant. "We no leave without Jim!"

*"Non,"* the Vulcan said simply. "We shall power up the Janus Gate from space and see if that dismays our enemies."

"Mr. Spock," Uhura said in urgent Vulcan. "If the Shechenag are telling us the truth about fighting a war for nine millennia, maybe *they* are the original inhabitants of Tlaoli. Maybe this Gate belongs to them."

"I have considered that possibility," Spock replied in his native language. "But the ancient Tlaoli people left this Gate for use by anyone who followed them. It would not be logical for them to chase away those successors now, especially if they could simply deactivate the Gate they built." He switched to the more guttural sounds of Tellerite. "I suspect these are not the aliens who built the Gate, but rather the enemies against whom it was once used. That would explain both their fear of using it, and their conviction that it cannot undo the disruptions it causes in the timeline."

The older Chekov cleared his throat. "So you don't think they really know how to deactivate this device?" he asked Spock in slow but passable Tellerite. "All they can do is try to barricade it from us?"

"That is my belief," Spock said.

"And if we cannot destroy their barricade by powering the Janus Gate from space?" asked the older Sulu, also in Tellerite, "What will we do then?"

Spock swept a measuring glance across the Shechenag, with their menacing cybernetic armor and the detachable robots now being arranged in a protective circle around the Janus Gate itself. He paused, then deliberately switched back to English again so all of them could understand his next words. "In that case, we will be forced to *attack* our problem more directly."

# Chapter Two

"YOUR SON ISN'T HERE," Kirk told his father. A flutter of burning cloth, made feather-light by the flames consuming it, drifted down between them to temporarily illuminate George Kirk's hard, determined face. *He's not as tall as I remember.* But he looked exactly as angry.

"He got on board just before you closed up," the elder Kirk insisted. The flames between them guttered down to amber pinpricks in the older man's eyes. "He's fourteen, just a little over a meter and a half, with a smart mouth. You must have seen him."

Kirk didn't try to hide the irritation on his face, although years of practice let him hide the emotion in his voice behind a crisp tone of command. "I didn't say I hadn't seen him, I said he wasn't here." He turned away to flip Maione's body and pat it down in search of weapons he could use if the Vragax returned. Not much to his surprise, none were left. "We sent him back to the embassy after the shuttle went down."

George Kirk had already begun to copy Kirk's weapons check on the other bodies nearby. "And you didn't send anyone with him?"

*Was he always this irreverent with his commanders?* "We didn't exactly have anyone to spare." Although maybe if one of them had come with him, that man would have been spared—would have kept Kirk out of the hands of the Vragax guerrillas—would have gotten them to the embassy in time to make everything different.

*But everything is already different.* The thought froze Kirk with his hand on a dead man's hip. *I'm here this time. I'm delaying my father.* He spun on George, suddenly shaken by the prospect of disrupting his own history. "Did you check the buildings?"

The other man jerked a look at him over one shoulder. "What?"

"The buildings," Kirk insisted, climbing to his feet and hauling up the meager gear he'd been able to salvage. "Between here and the embassy. Did you search any of the buildings?"

George was already jamming an extra phaser and a short string of sonic grenades into his belt. "I was following the shuttle." An awkward pause silenced him only briefly. "I didn't want to be delayed."

*Then when did you find me?* Kirk realized with a

sick, almost youthful panic that he wasn't exactly sure how his father had located him that night. He'd always assumed George had noticed some commotion that had led him to the armed Vragax who had cornered his son, or that he had stumbled across the imminent assassination through some stroke of unbelievable luck while on his way from the embassy launch pad to the crash site. He'd also always worried that his father's refusal to go back for Maione and the others had meant he was a self-centered son of a bitch who had found what he came for and couldn't be bothered with anything else. For some reason, it had never occurred to Kirk that his father had actually covered the entire distance to the downed shuttle and searched for him there before turning back toward the embassy. And after ending his blistering tongue-lashing with the words, "Your mother is *never* going to know about *any* of this, you understand?" George Kirk never spoke of that night again. Haunted by the thought of Maione, Leone, and all the others he'd left behind to face the Vragax alone, his son had shamefully followed the father's example.

At least now Kirk knew that no one had abandoned the shuttle's crew. George Kirk had found them, and he'd been just as helpless to save them as his son.

Wrenching his gaze away from the scattered bodies, Kirk motioned his father to join him at the rear of the shuttle. "We sent him back toward the embassy." It somehow made the deception easier when he spoke of himself in the third person. He could function as a captain then, reacting to the situation in front of him and taking the necessary action, and not just as the adult doppelganger of a terrified fourteen-year-old boy. "If you didn't come across him on your way out here, then he either made it back to the embassy—"

"There isn't much of an embassy to go back to."

"—or he's still out there somewhere."

Kirk didn't have to see the look of frustrated disgust on his father's face to know it was there. "I just hope he had enough sense to stay out of sight. The Vragax aren't being too particular about who they shoot right now."

Kirk slung the rifle half-readily across his front and left the shuttle's protective shadow before the urge to backhand his companion drove him to do something he was sure to regret. "He's not stupid," he assured his father without even bothering to waste a glare on him. "And he doesn't want to die any more than you do."

George Kirk fell into step beside him with a skeptical snort. "Sometimes I wonder."

They made better time together than Kirk had alone. Leapfrogging each other down the lengths of empty street, one always keeping watch while the other moved, they tugged on every door they passed, darted furtive looks inside every broken window. Kirk appreciated George's practicality—he didn't waste time kicking in locked doors or investigating intact windows. He might understand little else about his son, but he knew the boy wasn't capable of breaking in anywhere that wasn't already wide open. He just didn't have the strength or the skills.

For himself, Kirk struggled to call up some memory of the streets he'd run down that night, some distinguishing feature of the building where he'd finally been caught. Shouldn't such a seminal event have left indelible images in his brain? He had dreamed about the small, dark room where he'd tried to hide almost nightly for seven months. For years afterward, he could have drawn the pattern of blood and war paint and braids on the Vragax who'd finally cornered him. Yet now that his young life might actually depend on it, he couldn't even remember if the outside of the building was concrete, brick, or wooden shingle.

*Was I even gone this long? Shouldn't my father have found me by now?* That thought had been gnawing at him since they'd left the shuttle crash. What if his presence here had irrevocably altered the timeline? He already knew that no one had been with his father when George Kirk appeared like an avenging angel and killed the four Vragax surrounding his son. No one had come back with them to the embassy, no one had covered the last of their escape. Now that he was here—not only as an adult, but as George Kirk's nominal commander—Kirk wasn't even sure he could stand by and let the security officer shoot down the four natives without at least giving them a chance to surrender. He was just too confident that the two of them together could save the boy without having to resort to that kind of bloodshed.

*But what if you're wrong? What if it's already too late?*

George's urgent hiss knocked Kirk out of his reverie. Jogging up to meet him in an open doorway, Kirk barely caught sight of the older man until he was right on top of him, and then had to drop into an abrupt crouch at his side to avoid tripping over him altogether. George didn't seem to notice. He caught at Kirk's shoulder to direct his attention, then pointed with the muzzle of his rifle as though it were an extension of his own arm, into the blackened interior of the building beyond the doorway. "I hear voices upstairs." He mouthed the words almost directly into Kirk's ear, passing scarcely enough breath to make them audible. "And somebody's crying."

Kirk couldn't even feel indignant that his father would assume his son was huddled in the dark somewhere weeping. He'd been sobbing when he left Maione and the others at the shuttle that night, and hadn't been able to stop crying until several hours after his father had found him and dragged him back to safety. He was just grateful for the darkness now, so that the embarrassed heat in his face wouldn't give away how ashamed he still was of that weakness.

"I'll go first," George continued. "Keep me in sight, but wait for my signal."

George counted off *one, two, three* with the fingers of one hand, and they swung into the open doorway on *three* as though they'd drilled the maneuver together for months. Kirk blinked hard at the darkness, willing his eyes to adjust, and finally isolated a deeper length of black curving up along one wall. A stairway. George was halfway up it already, silently waving Kirk to follow as he eased around the first landing and peered up toward the second floor. Featureless doors lined the downstairs lobby, each sporting a bright metal plate engraved with Grexxen number pips on the wall immediately next to the doorknobs. An apartment building, then. Or maybe an office complex. Kirk padded up the stairs behind George as silently as possible, listening for the voices his father had followed, and one voice in particular.

The crying was more evident once they rounded the stairwell onto the plushly carpeted second floor. But it was a female, her sobs desperately muffled, and the voice that shushed and tutted to her was neither human nor threatening. "It's not him," Kirk whispered, even as his eyes strayed down the long hallway to the familiar door yawning open at the end. "He wouldn't have gone near them."

He didn't go near them. He hadn't known they were there. He'd simply run as far from the stairwell as he could, passing all the apartments and alcoves and closets, and ducked through that open door into an office whose boxes and equipment he thought would lend him shelter. He'd even tried to lock the door, but was too blind with panic to figure out how.

A terrified scream from inside the nearest apartment made Kirk whirl and snap the rifle up to his shoulder. But instead of a Vragax raiding party, he saw only George Kirk through the opened door, kneeling atop an overturned desk with his gun aimed straight down at whoever had huddled underneath. "Shut up and listen to me," George said, calmly but firmly. "We're looking for a human boy."

"Commander, stand down!"

George spared Kirk only a brief glance out of the corner of his eye, not altering the gun's alignment by so much as a micron. "Begging the captain's pardon, sir, but I've been dealing with the Grexxen for more than a year now. You have only been here a short while."

*You have no idea how true that is.* "I'm still not going to let any officer under me brutalize the natives in the name of familial concern." He stepped up beside George and closed his hand around the barrel of the gauss rifle to make it clear he was prepared to disarm him if the older man forced the issue. "I said stand down."

The hesitation was slight—just enough to rankle Kirk's instincts as a captain, but not so long that he had to respond to the implied insubordination. Kirk found himself smothering a grin as his father climbed down off the desk and stepped grudgingly behind him. As much as George Kirk hadn't appreciated his son's rebellious streak, it wasn't his mother who had given it to him.

Slinging his own rifle onto his back, Kirk turned cautiously to the women huddled behind the big desk and tried to decide if he should squat down on their level or keep a prudent distance. They were both Kozhu, and obviously civilians, but the situation in Sogo city had been so crazy at the end that he wasn't sure if such distinctions meant anything anymore. "Do you speak English?" he finally asked, staying where he was on the other side of the desk.

The older of the two nodded. While her bronze-green face was wet from crying, it was the younger girl who choked volubly on her sobs, hands pressed against her mouth in an effort to keep silent. Kirk's heart thudded painfully with pity.

"We saw the boy." The older woman held the girl against her, and met Kirk's gaze with a dignity that left little room for fear. "Vragax chased him that way—" She jerked her chin toward the end of the hall. Toward the office with its boxes, where the young James Kirk had almost died. "—but when they left again, they left without him."

George was already running in the direction of her nod, calling, "Jimmy! Jim, where are you?" but Kirk stayed with the Kozhu women, going down to one knee after all. The young girl—no older than most of his yeomen—recoiled slightly, and he reached out to touch a reassuring hand to her arm without thinking about how such a gesture would be taken. She stared at him, copper eyes wide and lambent in the darkness, as though she'd just been comforted by a bear.

The older woman frowned gently at him, studying something in his expression or features. "The boy you want—he looks like you. He's your son?"

Kirk laughed softly and rubbed at his eyes. "No, not my son."

"Mine." The growl of anger in George's voice ignited every defensive instinct Kirk had developed over years of having to deal with the man. Turning a glare back at him, he'd just opened his mouth to suggest George Kirk leave his son behind if the boy caused him so much more trouble than he was worth. Then he saw the stark grief on the older man's face, naked and laced with terror in the dim light, and all his youthful defiance sank to the pit of his stomach like a stone.

"He's gone." George's voice betrayed none of the emotion on his face. "He's not there."

Kirk wondered if his father had just never looked like that when in front of his youngest son, or if Kirk had simply been stupid enough to believe only what he could hear in George's voice and not what he could see with his young eyes.

Pushing to his feet, he hauled his captaincy around him like a shield and let his mind race ahead to what came next. *React to the situation.* "What about blood?" If he wasn't in the room, there were limited options as to how he could have left it. "Was there any sign of a struggle?"

George Kirk looked down at his feet, obviously stilling his mind so he could interpret the details of what he'd seen. "Some stuff is knocked around, but there're no windows or equipment broken, no blood."

Then the Vragax hadn't killed him. They'd had the gun in his face, the alien's finger had all but depressed the trigger when George stepped in and brought the party to an ugly end. That little band of Vragax hadn't been working on any kind of larger agenda. They weren't going to drag Kirk somewhere else to do their killing, or take his body with him when they left. He was just one more outlet for whatever rage had boiled over in Sogo that night.

But if his father hadn't arrived in time to rescue him, and the Vragax didn't shoot him…then what? Where was the body, if not the boy?

He looked down at the Kozhu women behind the toppled desk. "You said the Vragax left without the boy. Did they say anything?"

She looked for a moment as though she might actually laugh, but instead she said slowly, as though speaking to a stupid baby, "Not to us. We are Kozhu. We hid from them." Then a certain amount of sympathy must have overweighed her sarcasm, because she added, almost grudgingly, "But they were frightened. One of them was crying and praying to his *beyli.*"

His personal god. Like a guardian angel, some force to protect him from evil spirits and their doings. No fourteen-year-old boy could have made a Vragax soldier so afraid.

George caught at his elbow, drawing him back away from the desk and the natives still hiding behind it. "Captain, sir…" He'd recovered what passed for his composure, looking once again only impatient and vaguely irritated. "We're wasting time here—it must not have been Jimmy they saw."

Kirk shook his head. "It was."

"You can't know that."

He snapped a sharp look at his father. "How many other human boys do you think are out there tonight?"

George didn't have a ready answer.

His anger cooled as quickly as it had flared, Kirk gazed absently down the hall, trying to intuit his own behavior in a set of past events that had never happened. "If he somehow got out of that room, he's headed for the embassy."

"I told you," George said tensely. "The embassy's in pieces."

"But he knows about the auxiliary shuttle pad," Kirk reminded him. "It's outside the embassy walls, and it's the only place that would still have shuttles to get you off-planet." In fact, it was the place from which he and George had fled Grex nineteen years ago, in the very last shuttle to leave the war-torn planet. "There's nowhere else for him to go."

George gusted a grumbling resignation. "A couple of my boys are holding the last transport. But they're not going to wait all night. We'd better hurry."

Yes, they would. But he couldn't help hesitating to glance down at the women, torn between the past he remembered and the future he was still hoping to create.

George followed his gaze only long enough to take his arm again and try to pull him away. "They are part of the native civilian population," the security man reminded Kirk stiffly. "Whatever old scores the

Kozhu and the Vragax have between each other, it isn't our problem now."

Variations on a theme. Kirk could have scripted the political argument that would follow, if only they'd had time to indulge in one. Except this time George wouldn't be able to dismiss Kirk's opinions as the delusions of an idealistic little boy. *I'm the captain now. I can do whatever I want to.*

Shaking his arm loose, he pinned the commander with a disapproving glare. "We made it our problem when we agreed to help them rebuild after the Orions were gone. If we turn our backs now, we're no better than the Orions."

"You're worse than the Orions." The woman's tired words shocked Kirk into silence, wounding something more basic in him than a simple political stand. Her weary eyes said she was just as dismayed by his innocence as his father. "They may have called us slaves, but they kept Vragax and Kozhu from killing each other in the streets. It wasn't until Starfleet gave us freedom that the killing began again." She sank back into the shadows, pulling the young girl tighter into her arms and making them both very small against the back of a shattered chair. "Go away now. Go look for your boy. We would rather wait here until the Orions return."

The shuttle flight from Tlaoli up to the *Enterprise* wasn't as bad as Sulu had anticipated.

It was much worse.

The cargo shuttle *Caroline Herschel* which Spock

had brought down to the planet was the same class as the *Edwin Drake,* the ship which had been thrown into the future with Sulu at its helm. Both ships had a normal passenger load of ten, but that was when they weren't carrying the heavy magnetic shielding that Scotty had installed to insulate their warp cores from Tlaoli's power-draining subspace fields. In order to evacuate the dozen people left stranded on the planet when the *Enterprise* had lost the use of its transporter, both shuttles had been emptied of all their nonessential equipment. Now they needed to add Spock, McCoy, and the duplicate copies of Chekov and Sulu to the passenger load. Even taking into account the lighter weight of a fourteen-year-old James Kirk, that put them so far over the *Herschel*'s carrying capacity that Sulu didn't even want to think about it.

They spent a frantic half hour under the menacing shadow of the Shechenag ship that had trailed them back from the caverns, emptying the cargo shuttle of everything they could wrench free. Passenger seats, bulkhead covers, even the emergency food and water supplies that they were never supposed to take off without—all of it went flying out the open hatchway. Remembering how he'd flown the Gorn shuttle back on Basaraba standing up, Sulu had even tried to get rid of his pilot's seat, but found that Starfleet's shuttle designers had hidden the control circuits for the inertial dampeners inside it. He settled for ripping away all of the upholstery and cushioning from its bare metal struts. With the soundproofing removed, he made the unpleasant discovery that the dampener's control panel emitted an annoying high-pitched whine, halfway between an unseen mosquito and an overloaded phaser.

Spock paused before settling down in the place where the copilot's seat had once been. "Do you believe you are competent for piloting duties, Mr. Sulu?" he asked. "In most circumstances you are a far better pilot than I, but if you are suffering from exhaustion or time-dilation effects…"

"I don't think I am, Mr. Spock," Sulu said, honestly enough. "I didn't get much sleep when I was on Basaraba, but whatever that healing chamber did to me back in the caves seems to have fixed that along with my ribs." It was true that his ribs were healed, without even an ache or twinge left to mark the place where a brutal blow from a Romulan weapon had broken his bones, and saved his life. But the weariness he'd felt back on Basaraba had been transformed by Tlaoli's alien healing chambers into something more than just a sense of having rested.

What Sulu actually felt right now was a sharp, crackling alertness, the kind that usually meant a spike of adrenaline had just jolted into his bloodstream. He would have chalked it up to trepidation about the upcoming shuttle flight, except that he didn't have the rapid pulse and sweaty palms and hollow feeling in his stomach that too many stress hormones produced. Maybe the ancient Tlaoli didn't just heal their recycled soldiers, he thought.

Maybe they also medically enhanced them for the next battle they were going to be sent through time to fight.

Or maybe the alien healing chamber just hadn't known how to repair his body's overstressed fight-or-flight response.

Spock acknowledged Sulu's response simply by handing him a length of lightweight polymer cord. "Your crash webbing was embedded in your seat's upholstery," said the Vulcan. "In case of an emergency, this will have to suffice."

Sulu knotted the cord from one bare metal strut to another, then back again a little farther down his thighs, trying to anchor himself securely enough to the seat that he couldn't be thrown away from the flight controls by unexpected tremors in Tlaoli's gravitational field. Spock took the cord from him when he was done, but since there was nothing left to lash himself to, the Vulcan simply braced himself in the far corner of the cockpit. Outside the shuttle, a wine-colored sunset was slowly staining the eastern side of Tlaoli's rusty sky. Sulu glanced curiously at the shuttle's chronometer and realized with a start that this was still the same day it had been when he'd been hurled into the future. The long rainy night and stressful day he'd spent on Basaraba must not have correlated to the same amount of time back at the *Enterprise.*

"Everyone's roped down in the cargo bay, too?" he asked Spock as he powered up the warp engines.

With the bulkhead covers removed to lighten *Herschel*'s weight, the roar of the thrust generators was much louder, too. Sulu didn't envy the fifteen people crowded into the back compartment.

"Yes." The science officer gazed out at the angular Shechenag aircraft that had hovered watchfully over them as they loaded into the shuttle. The alien ship was finally moving away from them, but it didn't disappear. Instead, Sulu noted, it began to systematically destroy the survey team's base camp, not with weapons fire or a bomb but simply by landing its immense weight on the storage tents, one by one. The cybernetic aliens apparently hadn't lied when they said they no longer engaged in war, but that didn't mean they couldn't still be ruthless in their determination to make sure the *Enterprise* crew did no further damage to the timeline here on Tlaoli.

Sulu opened his mouth to say something about that to Spock, then realized he was procrastinating. The shuttle's engines were as warmed up and ready as they would ever be. He took a deep breath, then brought *Herschel*'s vertical thrusters up to full power. The sound of the warp engines rose to an echoing roar in the back of the cargo bay, but the shuttle only managed to lurch a little way off the ground before losing momentum again, like a tethered animal hitting the end of its chain.

"Interesting," said Spock. "As soon as the thrusters lose contact with a hard surface, they no longer have enough power to accelerate us vertically. Perhaps we will need to leave one of the duplicated officers behind after all."

Sulu scanned his readouts, measuring engine output against gravitational pull, then darted a quick glance out through the reddening dusk. "I don't think we'll need to do that, sir," he said, and began to painstakingly work the shuttle around to the right without losing any of its lift.

When Spock had flown the *Herschel* down from the *Enterprise,* he hadn't landed at the base camp itself, the way Sulu had done with the *Drake.* As a pilot, the Vulcan was steady and workmanlike but not particularly talented. Faced with Tlaoli's unreliable gravitational shifts and jagged terrain, he had opted to put the shuttle down on the edge of the windswept karst outside the towers surrounding the base camp. It had been a fortunate decision, leaving plenty of airspace off to starboard for Sulu to now maneuver in. There might be a bump or two along the way, he thought as he aimed the shuttle toward the clearest line of sight, but hopefully nothing bad enough to breach *Herschel*'s hull and make her unspaceworthy.

With another deep breath, Sulu transferred the shuttle's thrust from purely vertical to a slightly more upward-angled vector. With less energy devoted to fighting gravity, more of the engine's energy could be converted into motion. Before it could begin falling back to ground, the *Herschel* began to surge forward, gathering speed as it went. It was still no more than a handspan above the ground, and Sulu could hear the scrape of brittle shrubs and projecting rocks against the shuttle's tough duranium belly. He didn't take his eyes off the speed and altitude gauges, one of which was moving faster than he'd expected, the other of which seemed stubbornly stuck on its original value. Even with the warp engines powered up to their maximum level, he could hear the startled and questioning lift of voices from the back compartment as his passengers endured the brushes and bumps.

"There are several large rock formations ahead of us, at a distance of approximately sixteen thousand meters," Spock informed him in a calm and measured voice. It might have reassured Sulu more to hear the Vulcan science officer sound so normal if he hadn't known that Spock could speak just as calmly even when he was facing certain death. "We will need at least thirty-five meters of additional elevation to provide clearance."

"We'll get it." Sulu had already begun converting their horizontal thrust back to vertical by using the shuttle's own momentum as the catalyst to tip the balance between gravitational pull and upward lift. By slowly nudging *Herschel*'s nose so that it angled up into the darkening Tlaoli sunset, he had managed to raise the shuttle a full ten meters off the ground. If they could just overtop the rocks Spock had noted ahead of them, they'd have nothing but clear air ahead of them and plenty of time to trundle their way up to the *Enterprise.* But the thrust conversion was an excruciatingly slow process, and it wasn't being helped by the frictional drag of the occasional karst moundtops they were still brushing across.

"Thirteen thousand meters," Spock said. Sulu glanced down at his velocity readout and frowned. Their speed had increased to six hundred kilometers per hour, giving them more momentum but also carrying them much faster toward a potentially deadly rendezvous with the karst monoliths whose dark silhouette had begun to obliterate the amethyst glow of sunset. He coaxed the shuttle into a little steeper angle and felt it shudder as it reached the outer envelope of lift that it could sustain. If he tried to angle upward any more steeply, the overloaded craft was going to fall right out of the sky. If that happened, even at the paltry twenty meters of altitude they had managed to gain so far, Sulu suspected not many of his roped-in crewmates would walk away from the crash.

"Nine thousand meters," Spock said calmly.

Sulu swept a glance across his controls, racking his brain for anything else he could do to lighten *Herschel*'s load, or add to its slowly building momentum. As a cargo shuttle, there were no weapons he could fire to create additional push and using the shields to ward away the rocks would only reduce the power output going to the thrusters. He almost wished the shields were already up, so he could turn them off and divert the freed power to their engines... and then Sulu suddenly knew what he could do.

*"Hang on!"* he yelled as loudly as he could, hoping the people back in the cargo bay could hear him.

He waited until he saw Spock brace himself more securely against the cockpit walls, then reached under his seat and fumbled for the switch that would deactivate *Herschel*'s inertial dampeners.

The reaction was immediate. Uncompensated gravitational forces slammed Sulu back into his metal chair frame and held him pressed there more strongly than any shock webbing could have done. He felt the pull of increasing acceleration in the muscles of his face and throat as he slowly wrenched his head around to read the shuttle's thrust. The difference was small, but crucial: Horizontal thrust had suddenly increased by ten percent. Sulu forced himself to alter the shuttle's angle of ascent slowly, oh so slowly, to keep the uncompensated inertial forces from tearing his passengers—and his copilot—away from their braced holds.

"Five thousand meters." Spock's voice hadn't varied even slightly in its measured tone, despite the fact that Sulu could see the muscles of his chest and shoulders knot as the Vulcan fought to keep from being thrown across the cockpit. Only his superhuman strength kept him in place now. "We still need an additional seven meters of altitude."

"It's coming." Sulu pushed the shuttle up to the brink of its lift envelope again, felt it shudder as it teetered on the ragged edge of staying aloft or plunging back to earth. Its nose wavered, seemed to duck—then one of Tlaoli's random little gravitational shifts suddenly jerked it up and sideways, adding a full three meters to its altitude.

For a long moment, the horizontal part of that jolt threatened to send the shuttle into an uncontrolled sidelong skid. Sulu had to drop the *Herschel*'s nose to keep it from rolling, losing back one of those precious meters to gravity in the process, but the upward jerk had also increased the shuttle's momentum enough to let him push the angle of its climb up another five degrees. He threw a quick glance at the altitude meter and knew with a veteran pilot's certainty that they were going to make it even before Spock said, "One thousand meters to the highest rock formations. It now appears we have sufficient altitude to clear them."

Sulu knew he was right, but he still held his breath as the dark pinnacles of limestone loomed beneath them, far closer than his piloting instincts said any solid object should be to a shuttle now moving at over one thousand kilometers per hour. The *Herschel* passed over them without a bump or scrape of sound, but the wake of air she dragged with her hit the rock formations hard enough to send ripples of turbulence surging out in all directions. Sulu nearly lost his seat as the shuttle bounced through the suddenly choppy air. He grimaced and fought against the continuing unbalanced pull of gravity to lean forward and reactivate the inertial dampeners. It was only after he felt his straining body relax into the stabilized gravitational field that he realized the torque he'd been exposed to had woken up a familiar dull ache in his rib cage. Apparently, the Tlaoli chambers hadn't completely healed the damage there.

"Thank you, Lieutenant," said Spock.

Sulu wasn't sure if the Vulcan science officer was commending him for his piloting or just for turning the inertial dampeners back on again. To be safe, he acknowledged the comment with merely a standard, "Aye, sir."

The *Herschel* continued to lumber upward slowly into the darkening red-violet sky, but now Sulu could ease her back from the precarious edge of her lift envelope and let her ascend as slowly and gracefully as a hawk circling on a thermal draft. The higher they climbed, the less Tlaoli's gravity dragged on them and the more thrust he could devote to rising vertically. The inertial dampeners smoothed out most of the continuing gravitational jolts, allowing Spock to extricate himself from his uncomfortably cramped position in the corner of the cockpit, and move forward to scan the copilot's instruments. Although many of them displayed the warning red that meant Tlaoli's subspace interference had exceeded their maximum error levels, the shuttle's homing transponder still showed a clear vector on its screen.

"Once we reach the edge of the atmosphere, we will need to alter course toward the ecliptic plane in order to rendezvous with the *Enterprise,*" Spock informed him. Around them, the sky was darkening with more than the approach of night. The increasingly bright twinkle of stars above the rusty fringe of Tlaoli's horizon told Sulu they were in the upper stratosphere now and would soon reach the point where the air was thin enough to let them safely engage the warp drive. He cut back on the thrusters to keep from overloading them, and began banking the shuttle toward an ecliptic orbit.

"Are you finished torturing your passengers?" asked a Russian-accented voice from the passage connecting the cockpit to the cargo bay. Sulu didn't bother to look around to see which version of Chekov had disobeyed Spock's orders to stay in back until they reached the *Enterprise*. The caustic words were enough to identify him.

"Pavel, you're probably the only one aboard who feels tortured when someone saves your life," said a deeper and much more familiar voice. Despite himself, Sulu felt a small shudder crawl up between his shoulder blades. There had been no time, after the Shechenag captured and herded them through the caverns of Tlaoli, to really absorb the fact that he was not the only version of Sulu in the group. Now that it had time to sink in, Sulu found himself torn between intense curiosity and equally intense shyness, as if there were some point of etiquette that said he shouldn't be allowed to know what he would be like a few decades from now.

He stole a furtive glance at the middle-aged man who had joined the older Chekov in the cockpit door, and was a little startled by how few physical changes he saw, aside from the lines at the corners of his eyes. The older man had the same trim build, dark hair and dark eyes that Sulu saw in the mirror every day, but there was still something indefinably different about him. Sulu couldn't tell if it was the erect way he carried himself, or perhaps just the confidence that let him smile so wryly at his younger self, but somehow there was no doubting that *this* version of Sulu had earned his promotion to starship captain. Even if they managed to alter the future and avoid the Gorn conquest of space, Sulu thought wistfully as he returned his gaze to his instruments, this was still the man he hoped he would turn into.

The older Sulu leaned over his shoulder and ran a practiced eye across the instrument panel to check their course. "Aren't we going to reconnoiter the Shechenag's main ship before we head back to the *Enterprise?"* he asked, in a voice that somehow managed to imply that it would be a very good idea to do so without actually impinging on Spock's nominal position as commander of the landing party.

"The Janus Gate creates sufficient subspace interference that our instruments here are useless, Captain." Sulu wasn't sure if Spock was deliberately acknowledging the other Sulu's superior rank by using his title, or if it was just a logical way of distinguishing the two different versions of the pilot from each other. "I had planned to conduct a long-range surveillance from the *Enterprise."*

The older man made a noncommittal noise. "The Shechenag might take any approach as a sign we intended to engage them in battle."

"Or at least were disobeying their orders to leave the system," Sulu added tentatively.

"Well, we can at least do a visual inspection." Chekov leaned into the cockpit and jerked a thumb toward the starboard side of the cockpit window. "There's the Shechenag ship, right over there."

It wasn't easy to see at first, but Chekov was right. A shadow of solid black brushed out the star-studded glitter of outer space, on a track that would soon intersect with their own. Sulu cut the *Herschel*'s thrust and mentally cursed his dependence on instruments to orient himself to objects in space. Even though he knew his proximity alerts and sensors were malfunctioning, he hadn't thought to replace them with a thorough visual scan of the sky.

Apparently, the Shechenag didn't feel a need to light their starships from outside for safety the way all Federation vessels were required to be illuminated except in times of war. In fact, there was almost no evidence of light on the ship at all—no windows or portholes or even rings of docking lights to mark the entrances to the shuttlebays it presumably had. If the older Russian hadn't caught sight of it, they might have missed the alien ship entirely despite its massive size and slow movement. Either the cybernetic aliens saw in wavelengths other than the common visual spectrum humanoids tended to use, or they depended on their own instruments even more so than Sulu did. Which made Sulu wonder what would happen to them if they stayed in orbit around Tlaoli for too long.

"What's it doing?" his older counterpart asked after they had watched the ship for a few minutes.

Chekov snorted. "Besides moving through space, not much that I can see."

"No, it's the *way* it's moving." Sulu had noticed it, too, the subtle cycle of deceleration, drift, and acceleration that the Shechenag ship displayed on its slow orbit around Tlaoli. "It looks as if it's slowing down to do something every so often, then moving on again."

"Vulcans cannot see as well in the dark as humans do," Spock said calmly. "Lieutenant Sulu, if you would extinguish the cockpit lights—"

Sulu found the small dial on the *Herschel*'s instrument panel and dimmed both his displays as well as the overhead lights. It took his eyes a moment to adjust to the intense darkness of space, but when they did the pattern of the Shechenag ship suddenly made perfect sense.

"They're dropping satellites!" he blurted.

"Or mines," Chekov said.

A dozen of the tiny objects strung out like dimly glowing pearls behind the main ship, tracing the curve of its orbit around the nightside of Tlaoli and back toward its retreating sunset terminus. The detached objects weren't the only things glowing, either. Strands of light as iridescent as spider silk connected each satellite to the next, stringing them into a necklace that seemed to be held together by electromagnetic force rather than any physical agent.

"It's an integrated network," the older Sulu said quietly. "Once it's installed around the entire planet, it will probably generate some kind of defensive array."

Chekov grunted curt agreement. "If it's anything like the kind we installed around some of our colonies once the Gorn started attacking from space, it won't let ships pass either way once it's been activated. And," he added grimly, "it looks to me like it's being activated as they install it."

# Chapter Three

"HEY, where does this go?"

Chekov automatically detoured the couple of steps necessary to crane a look up the access ladder Kirk had leaped onto and gleefully begun to climb. He immediately felt stupid for having gone through the motions. "Uh..." He barely knew where the main corridors and turbolift shafts led on board this ship, much less all the auxiliary conduits and passageways. Trying to cover his uncertainty, he hauled the boy back down to the deck with a little more force than necessary. "It just goes up to the next deck. It's a maintenance access."

Just in case he hadn't sounded uncertain enough, his older self snorted with unconcealed disdain from where he waited with Sulu on the other side of the corridor. Chekov bit down hard against a flush of embarrassment and tried to act as though he hadn't heard. Bad enough that Spock had given him responsibility for leading their guests to a set of quarters he'd never seen before—it was far worse to have one of them be a man who must know every insecure and self-castigating thought that passed through his head. Waving to Kirk a little impatiently, Chekov said, "It doesn't go anywhere interesting. Come on."

Kirk tossed one last look up the ladder, but followed readily enough when the small group continued down the corridor. Hurrying a little to reclaim his place alongside Chekov, he asked cheerfully, "You have no idea where it goes, do you?"

Chekov didn't look at him. "No."

Kirk nodded as though that confirmed something he'd long suspected. "Do you actually serve on board this ship?"

Chekov darted an irritated glance at the boy, then softened when he saw Kirk's playful grin. Embarrassed all over again, he admitted quietly, "I'm new," and hoped the Chekov behind them wouldn't have anything to add.

"Does that mean we're gonna get lost?" Kirk actually sounded pleased by that prospect, glancing down the next intersection with an air of boyish adventure. "How many days do you think we can wander the decks without going past the same place twice?"

Judging from Chekov's experience so far, quite a few. "We're not going to get lost." He tried to make the assertion sound confident instead of desperately hopeful. But then the older man behind him muttered something to Sulu that Chekov didn't quite hear, and he felt obliged to add, "It just might take us a few extra minutes to get anywhere we're trying to go."

In retrospect, he probably should have worked harder at making Spock understand his lack of familiarity with the ship's layout when the first officer saddled him with this assignment. But he'd been the last one on an examination bed, in the midst of blowing as hard as he could into the respiratory sensor Nurse Chapel had just handed him, and Spock had lingered in the doorway only long enough to announce, "Ensign Chekov, please see that our guests are settled in these temporary billets," before dropping a padd on the desktop and exiting as brusquely as he'd arrived. At the time, it hadn't seemed appropriate to leap up and chase the first officer out into the hallway just to exclaim, "But I can't even find my *own* quarters half the time! We'll be wandering the ship for hours!"

Now, he was starting to regret that earlier inaction.

"Apparently, in this alternate timeline, crew quarters are no longer on deck six."

The sound of his own voice—but colder, and not as heavily accented—sent an unpleasant shiver up Chekov's spine. It was as if he were hearing his most critical inner demons projected aloud. Halting, he turned back the way they'd just come to find the older version of himself gesturing with mock courtesy down a side corridor that Chekov had just walked blithely past. He recognized it immediately as the route they needed to take to reach the turbolift for the crew's quarters, and wanted to kick himself for not making the realization just a few seconds earlier. The expression of tolerant sympathy on Captain Sulu's face didn't make him feel any better about it, nor did being forced to step in front of both men to resume his lead position as they turned the corner. "Excuse me, sirs..."

Just when he thought the worst of it was over, that cold artifact of his own voice suggested, very close to his ear, *"Vuey mogli vcegda tyanytch nebolshouye karti vashei rukye..." You could always draw a little map on your hand.*

A sharp thump told him that Sulu had cuffed his first officer on the shoulder, apparently with the prosthetic hand McCoy had fitted him with not an hour before. "Pavel, stop harassing the boy."

The elder Chekov didn't seem terribly concerned by his commanding officer's reprimand. "If we left it up to him, we'd be wandering in the desert for forty years."

Sulu snorted. "Do I have to remind you that you *were* him just twenty-five years ago?"

"No," the other man snarled curtly. "It's bad enough that *he* reminds me."

No one said anything after that on the short turbolift ride up to deck six, not even Kirk, who occupied himself by peering into every maintenance panel he had time to flip open during the trip. Inspired perhaps by his own mortification and his willingness to be done with this unpleasant duty, Chekov found the empty billet described in Spock's directions almost as though he actually knew where they were going. He keyed in the access code, then stepped back to clear the entrance as the door slid obediently open.

"I'm afraid nothing's been removed from the previous occupant," he explained, remembering that, too, from the orders spelled out on Spock's padd. "Lieutenant Tormolen died only a few days ago, and with everything that's happened…"

An expression he wasn't sure how to interpret moved wistfully across Sulu's face, as though he'd just been reminded of something he hadn't thought about for many years. "We understand. Thank you."

Chekov stole a glance at his older self's back as the man shouldered past him into the room without bothering to excuse himself or say good-bye. *What did you expect?* Chekov chided himself, feeling embarrassed and angry all over gain. *Some kindly pearls of wisdom about which future girlfriend to watch out for?*

No, of course not…But he wouldn't have minded at least some indication that he could stand to look at himself without being disgusted.

Chekov realized he'd lingered a moment longer than necessary when Sulu smiled at him gently and tossed a nod back over one shoulder. "Don't mind him. He's just sulking because we didn't let him kill himself." A snort from the room behind him was the only indication he'd been overheard. If anything, the captain's smile softened with even greater fondness.

"Thank you for everything, Ensign. I'm sure we'll be seeing each other again later." Then he stepped back into the dead crewman's quarters and let the door slide shut behind him.

The moment they were alone, Kirk remarked conversationally, "My future's better than yours."

*My future's just scary.* Chekov turned to look at him, abruptly remembering the instructions McCoy had given him and the other members of the landing party after Spock had left. "We should get some sleep ourselves."

Kirk tossed him a puckish grin. "Can you find your quarters from here?"

Even depressed and half-exhausted, Chekov managed to dignify the boy's remark with a satisfactorily offended glower. "Yes, I can find my quarters. Most of the time."

"Okay." Kirk's grin widened conspiratorially. "Can you find *my* quarters?"

Chekov brought them to a halt in the middle of the corridor. "I am *not* taking you to the captain's cabin."

"Just for a minute!"

"I don't even have the codes to get in."

"I bet I could figure them out." Kirk slid around in front of him, looking smugly pleased with himself and for all the world like the kind of boy who could go anywhere he wanted. "It's probably something stupid, like the birthday of my favorite dog."

Chekov didn't even know that Captain Kirk had owned a favorite dog. "No."

"But it's *my* room," Kirk protested. "Can't I order you or something?"

"Not for another twenty years."

Although he heaved a dramatic sigh of resignation, Kirk's smile remained undimmed, and he fell into step beside Chekov again as though he hadn't really expected a different answer. "Can we at least go see some other part of the ship? I'm hungry—we could go to the mess hall." When Chekov rolled his eyes at the suggestion, Kirk caught at his arm and dragged him to a stop with a little laugh. "Oh, come on! I've barely eaten since I got here, and I can't believe you're not going to show me the whole ship, and besides I'm *way* too excited to sleep."

The mention of food—no matter how fleeting—reminded Chekov's stomach that he hadn't eaten since their arrival at Tlaoli, either, and now the empty cramping was giving his fatigue a run for its money. Since they'd all been ordered by McCoy to get a good meal in addition to as much sleep as possible, he supposed it didn't really matter in what order those events occurred. He motioned Kirk back toward the turbolift with a sigh. "Lucky for you, I know how to find the rec hall."

Heads turned with the usual casual interest when they entered, but a few crew members looked a little longer than Chekov was used to. He found himself wondering how far word had spread about what had happened planetside, and how many of the people staring knew who the boy with him was, and how many others couldn't even guess. They were in the middle of a shift, which meant only a handful of crew were actually present. Still, Chekov tried to hold himself erect and unself-conscious as he led Kirk over to the banks of food slots. Whatever gossip might spring up from this public glimpse of the boy who would be their commander, at least no one could say that Chekov was embarrassed to be saddled with him.

Tapping Kirk's shoulder to retrieve his attention from where it had strayed toward a three-dimensional chess game going on nearby, Chekov explained the food ordering system by keying up his own dinner as an example. Kirk watched the steps keenly, then stepped up to the menu screen with all the delight of a boy given his first 3-D entertainment set. He was still scrolling through the choices when Chekov's food arrived, but seemed to interrupt himself abruptly by pointing to one particular entry and asking, "What's this?"

Chekov glanced at the screen. It was part of the Northern Africa menu, and he couldn't even begin to pronounce the name. "I have no idea."

As though that were precisely the answer he'd hoped for, Kirk promptly punched in that selection and stepped back to wait with a self-satisfied grin on his face. Chekov could only shake his head in wonder. "I cannot believe you're intending to eat something when you have no idea what it is."

"Are you kidding?" Kirk looked honestly surprised at his companion's diffidence. "It'll be fun!"

Whether or not it was fun, it was certainly colorful. A riotous patchwork of bright reds, greens, and yellows decorated a plate that had been draped with what Chekov initially took as a sheet of linen napkin. Closer inspection revealed it to be some sort of pale, clothlike bread. A second piece of the same spongy material had been neatly folded on a smaller plate beside the first. Chekov had to admit that it all smelled very rich and wonderful, but he was still skeptical of anything that didn't come out of the machine in the company of a fork and knife.

"See?" Kirk said as he slid into an empty seat as though already accustomed to doing it every day. "Your food is all just sort of white and sitting there. Mine is interesting and brightly colored."

Chekov took the seat across from him. "Venomous animals are also brightly colored," he pointed out.

Kirk made a disapproving face. "Don't be such a hen. It's on the menu—" He tore off a section of the separate napkin-that-wasn't and used it to scoop up a handful of food. "—so it's not like it can kill me."

Chekov watched the boy dive into his food with a fascination bordering on amazement. It wasn't necessarily the flavor of the food Kirk enjoyed, he realized, it was the experience—the opportunity to do something he'd never done before, even if it was something as simple as eating a North African meal with his hands. He supposed he shouldn't be surprised. After all, if the man who commanded a starship on the very edges of the frontier didn't derive excitement from all things new and different, what was he doing on the frontier at all?

Chekov glanced down at his own considerably less adventuresome meal. *Am I sure I have what it takes to be a starship commander?*

Coughing once, Kirk abruptly dropped his bread-napkin into the center of his plate and clapped both hands to his mouth. Chekov looked up at him in alarm as the boy's eyebrows climbed toward his hairline and his face darkened to an appalling shade of red. "Are you all right?"

Nodding vigorously, Kirk groped for the glass of milk he'd ordered with his dinner, and finally managed to squeak, "Hot!" just before gulping down a series of desperate mouthfuls.

Chekov laughed. "I warned you."

"No, no—it's good!" But even that assurance collapsed into a strangled little cough before it could sound too convincing, and Kirk emptied the rest of his milk in a couple of quick swallows. Still laughing, Chekov pushed his own water across the table and into Kirk's reaching hand.

Finishing only half of the water, Kirk sat back with a loud exhalation of relief, then cocked his head at Chekov as though only just putting a finger on something that had been bothering him for a while. "He never smiles."

"Who?" Chekov asked.

"You." An impatient scowl wrinkled his young face, and he waved his hand in frustration at not having the pronouns to easily discuss what they were all in the midst of. "The other you. Him." He leaned forward to replace the half-empty water glass on Chekov's side of the table. "Even when he says something funny, it's like he knows it's funny, but he doesn't really care."

Chekov felt his own smile evaporate, and struggled not to let it sink into a frown as he toyed with the suddenly unappetizing food on his plate.

"Does it bug you?" Kirk asked, blunt in his youthful sincerity. "Knowing you might end up being..." Words failed him again, and he shrugged. "...somebody you feel like you aren't?"

Chekov returned the shrug. "A little." But that wasn't really true, and he still felt awkward lying to the boy. "A lot," he finally admitted. He dropped his fork onto his plate and pushed it off to one side. "But maybe knowing it's a possibility will help me prevent it from happening." It didn't sound any more convincing now than when he said it to himself.

Kirk gathered another more cautious mouthful of food, and chewed it carefully while he thought. "Maybe it's not good for us to know too much about who we're going to be. I mean, I keep wondering if I'm gonna be *me* for the next twenty years, or if I'm always going to be thinking I ought to be doing this thing or that thing not because I want to, but because it's what a guy who's supposed to be a great starship commander would do."

It hadn't occurred to Chekov until just then that

seeing a brilliant future for yourself could be just as intimidating as seeing one you didn't like. "Captain Kirk became a great starship commander without knowing anything about his future. You'll become him just by being who you are."

Kirk looked at him frankly. "So does that mean you have to become Mr. Sunshine?"

"I don't know...I don't think so." Chekov said it more because he needed to believe it than because he honestly felt it was true.

"You know what I think?" Down to the bread-napkin lining of his dinner, Kirk began tearing it into individual colorful strips that he could roll up and pop in his mouth. "I think if we can fix the timeline so that the Gorn don't take over the Federation—I think you'll stay a nice guy because the world won't have gotten so crappy."

Chekov studied this young man with all his nascent greatness, and asked, in as neutral a tone as he could muster, "You're not afraid of going back?"

Kirk thought about that long enough to give an honest answer. "A little." Then, with that same quick-silver smile, "A lot. But if I don't go back, there's so much bad stuff that will happen, and so much good stuff that never will." He waved expansively around the now nearly empty rec hall. "I won't get to have this great ship, and you guys won't get to be my minions."

Grinning, Chekov lifted his eyebrow in mock dismay. *"Minions?"*

"Sorry. I meant my brave and loyal crew," Kirk said with patently false sincerity. "I wouldn't want you guys to end up with some other crummy captain like the one who screwed things up with the Gorn. Besides—" He leaned forward on his elbows with a smile so wicked it made his eyes twinkle. "I can't wait to find out how me as a great starship commander is getting along with my dad."

She had actually escaped Tlaoli.

The reality of having finally left the planet where she had spent so many frantic and helpless hours took a long time to sink into Uhura's consciousness. She found herself reaching up to where her helmet carbide used to be whenever she needed to turn on the light in her quarters, and when she put her normal uniform on, the first thing she thought was that it wasn't going to do much good if that alien chill swept through the caves again. Even after two hours of getting cleaned up and debriefed and taking an all-too-brief nap, Uhura found herself wondering what the next crisis in the ice caverns would be.

Her subconscious fear that she hadn't really left the alien planet worried Uhura enough that she mentioned it to Dr. McCoy when she went to get his medical clearance for the early return to duty that Spock had requested. In response, she got a long lecture on the relationship of sleep to residual post-stress tension, as well as a restorative dose of melatonin, time-released glucose, electrolytes, and fluids. Even as he prepared the nutritional supplement, Dr. McCoy grumbled about the order that had woken her early and summoned her back to bridge duty.

"It's those damned Vulcan chromosomes of his," he declared. "Spock thinks because he can go for days without sleep, so can everyone else aboard this ship."

Uhura took the glass the doctor handed her, wrinkling her nose at its chalky look and sterile chemical smell. She refrained from pointing out that McCoy himself hadn't gotten any sleep yet, knowing that would only get her an irritated look and a harumph. Instead, she gulped down as much of her medicine as she could manage in one determined pull, then handed it back to him with a grimace.

"Couldn't you at least put some vanilla flavor into it?"

"I'm a doctor, not a bartender!" McCoy told her tartly. "And you need to finish *all* of that, Lieutenant, or I'm not going to clear you for duty."

"I think coffee would have worked just as well to keep me awake. And tasted a whole lot better." Uhura pinched her fingers on her nose and swallowed the rest of the nutritional supplement. Despite her protests, she could already feel her body responding to McCoy's concoction with a reassuring burst of energy. "Am I allowed to get a real breakfast on my way up to the bridge?"

"Only if you think Spock won't mind waiting another half hour for you to get there." McCoy's lips quirked at the face she made. "That's what I thought. Here."

Uhura took the tray he handed her and discovered it was a portable meal from the sickbay food dispensers, complete with a capped mug of steaming coffee. The fried-egg sandwich wouldn't have been her first choice for breakfast, but unlike Belgian waffles it had the benefit of being able to be consumed inside a turbolift. And after nearly two days of dry emergency rations and meager base camp meals, the chocolate croissant McCoy had added to the tray looked like heavenly ambrosia.

"Bless you, Doctor!" Uhura gave McCoy's cheek a peck as she slid off the examining table. The physician stepped back and muttered something indistinct, a tinge of red creeping up along his cheekbones. "Did you order a breakfast like this for Mr. Spock, too?"

"Spock!" That got her the harumph she'd avoided earlier. "He's just as bad as that grumpy version of Chekov. He wouldn't even let me check to make sure he wasn't exhausted. If he's eaten anything, mark my words...it was probably either an emergency ration bar or some Vulcan version of gruel."

Uhura left sickbay chuckling between hurried bites of biscuit and gulps of coffee. At the last minute, she remembered to make the turbolift stop at the sub-bridge ready deck, so she could dispose of the tray and swipe the crumbs off her red uniform before she reported for duty. The smell of coffee and chocolate must have clung to her strongly enough, though, to earn her a twinkling look from Chief Engineer Montgomery Scott, who was waiting for the turbolift on the back deck of the bridge.

"It's good to see *someone* taking the time to eat around here," Scott said, his voice booming loudly enough to carry back to the captain's chair. Uhura could see Spock standing beside the empty console, as he usually did when he was left in command of the bridge, but the Vulcan didn't appear to have noticed that Scotty's comment was intended for him instead of Uhura. The chief engineer snorted and rolled his eyes at Uhura, then stepped past her into the turbolift and told it, "Engineering."

Uhura paused as the turbolift doors hissed shut behind her, scanning the crewmen at the bridge stations. She recognized some of the faces from the night-shift: Lieutenant Tora Rhada at the helm and Sean DePaul at navigations, Elizabeth Palmer at communications and Richard Washburn at engineering. But the ship's chief astrobiologist, Lieutenant Commander Ann Mulhall, was manning the science station in place of the usual second-shift Science Officer Boma, and the security desk was occupied by the chief of security himself, Antonio Giotto. Unsure of whether Spock wanted her to relieve Palmer in the midst of her shift or carry out some other work detail, Uhura stepped forward and cleared her throat.

"Lieutenant Uhura reporting for duty, sir."

"Indeed," said Spock without turning around, as if he'd been aware of her presence all along. "I appreciate you taking the time to consume a meal before you reported, Lieutenant. It will save you the trouble of being harassed about your dietary requirements by various ranking officers of the ship."

Uhura bit her bottom lip to suppress a giggle. As usual, the Vulcan's comment was perfectly serious. And although Kirk or McCoy might have been able to tease him about that, it wasn't her place as a junior line officer to do so. "Do you want me to man the communications station, Mr. Spock?"

"No." The science officer turned toward her, and she could see now that he held a small mud-splattered instrument in his hands. "Lieutenant Palamas is still being treated in sickbay for the aftereffects of electrical shock. I require your expertise to cross-correlate the records you made down on the planet with Lieutenant Commander Mulhall's database of galactic archaeological artifacts."

Uhura came forward to take the visual translator from him, although she barely recognized the archaeological device now that it had been stripped of its bulky protective cover. "Are the records still intact?"

"Yes. I had Commander Scott remove the magnetic shielding himself, to guarantee nothing was damaged in the process." Spock's face looked a little more gaunt and sharply carved than usual, but nothing else about him betrayed the tense situation they were in. On the main viewscreen, Uhura could see the dark shadow of another spaceship blotting out the stars as it slowly orbited Tlaoli. It trailed a faint line of spider silk in its wake. Uhura realized that must be the Shechenag ship, setting up the network of defensive satellites Captain Sulu had told them about back on board the *Herschel.* She couldn't tell how many of those iridescent strands of force were already in place around Tlaoli, since the dusty garnet glow of its dayside outshone any that might have crossed it, but Uhura suspected there wasn't much time to waste. She glanced back up at Spock.

"Are you looking for any particular information from the Tlaoli records?"

The Vulcan lifted one eyebrow, but his face was otherwise so stolid that Uhura couldn't tell if he was expressing admiration for her efficiency or surprise that she had asked such an obvious question. "I wish to know if the ancient Tlaoli ever encountered a shield such as this when they fought the Shechenag, and, if so, whether they discovered a way to counteract it. Failing that, I wish to know where the Shechenag have come from and why it took them so long to reach Tlaoli after we arrived. Given their insistence on preventing any use of the Janus Gate, they seem to have left it oddly unprotected in an empty quadrant of space."

Uhura nodded and headed over to the science station, where Mulhall greeted her with a preoccupied nod. Uhura didn't hold that against her. All she really knew about the *Enterprise*'s chief astrobiologist was that Mulhall ate, slept, and breathed for her esoteric science specialty. Uhura didn't even try to pry her away from whatever query she was running through her database. Instead, she quietly set the archaeological translator on the science desk beside her and ran its leads into an unused data port, then began downloading its records of the Tlaoli written language into the ship's main computer so they could be translated more thoroughly than she and Palamas had managed down on the planet. Unlike the visual translator, the ship's logic circuits could reconstruct the rice-shaped phonemes that had been obliterated by cracks and tarnish on the walls of the Janus chamber. After a moment, the computer's artificial voice said quietly, "Translation 99.3 percent complete. Continue iterations for additional word discrimination?"

"How long will that take?" Uhura asked it.

"Four hours to achieve 99.9 percent completion."

"We'll go with what we've got." Uhura glanced up at Mulhall inquiringly. "Are you ready to start correlating, sir?"

The astrobiologist nodded again, but this time the full intensity of her pale-gray gaze was focused on Uhura and the translator. It was a little disconcerting. Mulhall was much taller than Uhura, tall enough that she hadn't even needed to adjust the tilt of Spock's display screen in order to use it. Her finely chiseled face held a strength and intelligence that suggested why she had risen to the rank of lieutenant commander, unusually high for a science specialist so young.

"How old do you estimate those written records are?" Mulhall asked, fingers poised over the keyboard to input Uhura's answer.

"We don't know." Uhura felt a flicker of annoyance at the incredulous look Mulhall gave her. "Our instruments weren't working all that well down on Tlaoli. All the geologists could tell was that the alien ruins were older than the caves above them. So they're at least several thousand years old and possibly millions of years older than that."

"Then we won't bother looking for an exact match," Mulhall said crisply. "We'll do a language derivation check. Give me a prioritized list of the ten most common grammatical elements in the language and I'll cross-reference that to every similar structure in our linguistic records."

It was Uhura's turn to look surprised. "Only ten? Wouldn't it be better to use more?"

The astrobiologist shook her head. "Linguistic studies have shown that it only takes six to seven matches to pin down a genetic relationship if it's really there. Once you start using less common language elements, you get too many false positives."

Uhura fed the request into the computer via the visual translator, and saw the flicker of response that immediately crossed Mulhall's display screen. "Will it cause problems if I do some searches on my translation while you run the cross-check?"

"Not until I get a match, and need to refine the linguistic derivation."

"Good." Uhura had been thinking about how she could search the translated Tlaoli writings for the information Spock wanted. Instead of selecting abstract concepts like "defensive shield" or proper names like Shechenag which might have changed through time, she'd decided it would be better to search for the discrete physical objects that would be mentioned if the Tlaoli military records contained any discussion of this type of warfare. She said, "Ship's computer: locate all variants of the following terms in the Tlaoli records: 'satellite,' 'space buoy,' 'orbital platform.' "

"Locating," the computer said, then was silent for a while. "There is only one usage of a term equivalent to any of those words. Translation follows: 'All of the other worlds and satellites we once occupied were lost, one by one, as the war continued for millennia.' Shall I continue?"

"No." Uhura glanced back over her shoulder at the viewscreen. They were now orbiting around Tlaoli's nightside, and the strands of force that marked the growing barricade around the ancient planet glimmered like frostfire in the darkness. They crossed and recrossed at a variety of angles, looking more than ever like a floating spiderweb. "Try locating all variants of the following terms: 'space blockade,' 'space network,' 'space quarantine.' "

"Locating." Another long pause. "There are no parts of the translation that correlate to any of those terms."

Uhura heaved a sigh. "All right. Then see if you can find a proper noun similar to Shechenag. Use a 30 percent differential in pronunciation to locate all possible variants."

"Locating. Word found in two hundred and forty-seven places." Uhura gave herself a mental thump on the head. Sometimes, the thing you thought was too simple to look for was actually the best. "Would you like verbatim translations of all instances where the word is used?"

"Can you compile a summary of those sections of the records, or are the instances scattered around too much to do that?"

"Two hundred and thirteen usages of the word 'Shechenag' are contained within nineteen percent of the text," the computer said. "It will take approximately fifteen minutes to compile a summary of that section. Of the remaining usages, twenty-three are scattered throughout the text and eleven are compressed into a very small passage at the end."

Uhura frowned, remembering the rough translation they had made down on the planet. The largest group of references to the Shechenag probably came from the historical section where the Tlaoli described their millennia-long war. Since the computer had already determined that no references were made in the text to satellites or space blockades, the blow-by-blow details of that ancient conflict might not be all that helpful now. The shorter section was more promising, since it was placed at the end of the text where the Tlaoli granted the use of the Janus Gate to anyone who might find it in the future. If it had occurred to them to add a warning there about their ancient enemies...

"I think I have a partial correlation," Mulhall said, without looking away from Spock's science monitor. "And if I'm right, I've got some intriguing cross-references popping up in a database of Andorian myths and legends. Can I merge your text records into my query now?"

"Give me one more minute," Uhura said. "Computer, mark the longer section of the records for future compilation. Translate the section at the end where the Shechenag are mentioned eleven times."

"Translating." This time, the computer's pause was long enough that Uhura could hear a rumble of voices coming from the security station as Giotto consulted Spock about something. She glanced over her shoulder, but saw nothing particularly alarming on the viewscreen. In fact, the Shechenag ship appeared to have come to a stop, leaving its spidery network less than half complete. "The section can be condensed as follows: 'Use of the Janus Gate should not be undertaken lightly. As we discovered during the war with the Shechenag, some changes made to our benefit in past battles resulted in a poorer future outcome. The likelihood of such inverse results can be predicted, but the Shechenag were never able to do this.

"'Many unrecoverable disasters were created in the timestream when the Shechenag stole our technology and tried to copy our chronological intervention techniques. In fact, the great interregnum in the war resulted from a Shechenag populist uprising to protest the use of time travel. Ever since that time, the

Shechenag sovereignty have tried to exterminate all use of time-slip devices, by themselves or by others.

"'We do not believe the Shechenag have now or ever will have the technology to destroy this Janus Gate, but the Shechenag sovereignty may attempt to prevent anyone else from using it as we do. Our homeworld lies on the farthest reaches of Shechenag space, in a region where they do not travel due to the risk of encountering other races whose behavior they cannot predict or control. But if the Janus Gate is used, the Shechenag may risk even such encounters in their zeal to protect the timeline. Use of the Janus Gate should therefore be made with adequate precautions against a Shechenag response, and with the understanding that such use may result in a declaration of war upon the user by whatever remains of the Shechenag Empire.'"

"Fascinating." The Vulcan's superior hearing must have let him absorb the computer's report from his position at the security station across the bridge. "That would explain why it took several days for the Shechenag to arrive and evict us from Tlaoli. However, it still does not answer the question of why they leave the planet undefended in their absence."

"I think I know the answer to that." Mulhall looked up from the science display screen, her strong-boned face alight with the intellectual satisfaction of having solved part of the Shechenag puzzle. "The closest match we've got to the Tlaoli language in our database is an obscure, post-technological civilization out past Andorian space. In trying to find out more about them, I ran across an old Andorian legend that seems to refer to Tlaoli itself."

"Indeed?" Spock turned to give them his full attention, although he didn't leave the security station. Alerted by his presence there, Uhura looked up at the viewscreen more carefully, trying to identify the threat Giotto and Spock must have identified there. "What does this legend say?"

"It's actually very similar to the Irish legends of Brigadoon, a magical town that appears and disappears," Mulhall said with an unexpectedly whimsical smile. "The Andorian storytellers claim there's a whole planet like that, in a quadrant so distant no one remembers its direction anymore. For thousands of years, according to the legend, no one can see or land on this planet, because it's shrouded in some kind of glowing ionic storm. But every so often the ionic storm calms down, and then the planet can be seen and landed on. If you visit the planet at those times, the story goes, you might be killed and eaten by monsters. Or, if you're lucky, you might regain your heart's lost desire." Mulhall made a slightly embarrassed face. "I'm not sure if that last part means much of anything. It's how Andorian storytellers usually like to end a legend."

"Getting your heart's lost desire could refer to the use of the Janus Gate to change an unfortunate decision you made in the past," Uhura pointed out. "And even if it's not monsters, there's certainly something down on Tlaoli that eats spaceships by draining their power supply, and kills them by dragging them out of orbit."

"You are quite correct, Lieutenant." Spock turned back to watch something on one of the security readouts, but his voice continued the conversation just as deftly even without his full attention. "Furthermore, if the glowing ion storm in the story were generated by a defensive barrier similar to the one which the Shechenag are currently erecting around Tlaoli, it may be that they do, indeed, protect the planet for long periods of time, until the Janus Gate manages to bring their barrier down. If the barrier failed shortly before we first arrived here with our landing parties—"

The Vulcan's voice cut off abruptly and Uhura saw his hand move in a blur too fast to distinguish. Milliseconds later, the familiar howl of red-alert sirens echoed through the ship.

"Evasive action, Mr. Rhada!" Spock's voice never sounded desperate, but it could rise to an insistent shout when circumstances seemed to warrant it. It did that now, telling Uhura everything she needed to know about the gravity of the situation. "All shields at full power, but do *not* fire phasers. Do you hear understand, Mr. Giotto?"

"I hear you, Mr. Spock," the security chief said grudgingly. "But if those aliens out there start firing at us—"

"I do not believe they will." Spock's gaze slanted back up toward the viewscreen, and Uhura's followed it. This time, however, she finally understood what she was seeing. The dark shadow of a Shechenag spaceship that appeared to be standing still against the stars—that was an optical illusion, caused by the alien ship's lack of lights and therefore of easy size reference. In actuality, Uhura realized with a start, the Shechenag ship wasn't standing still at all.

It was approaching the *Enterprise* head-on.

# Chapter Four

THE SHRIEK OF THE red-alert siren blasted through the bridge of the *Enterprise,* followed by an urgent cascade of voices as the crew reported in from their stations. It felt odd to Uhura not to be part of that disciplined response, to be merely a bystander on the bridge instead of an integral part of its functioning. All she could do was step back and keep a watchful eye on Ann Mulhall. Science specialists were rarely present on the bridge during times of crisis, and she wanted to make sure Mulhall didn't interfere with the flow of information by asking questions or making irrelevant comments. But the astrobiologist was silent, observing the crew with a fascinated eye as if they were some new species of aliens she had never seen before.

"Evasive maneuvers aren't working." That was

Lieutenant DePaul at navigations, watching both his own viewscreen and Rhada's as the pilot concentrated on shifting from one set of random orbital curves to another. The replacement helmsman had steady hands, but she was nowhere near as swift with her course changes as Sulu would have been, Uhura thought as she watched her.

"Shields up." Giotto angled a stubborn look up at Spock. "Main phasers targeted and ready to fire."

*"Wait for my signal."* There was never emotion in Spock's voice, but the clipped intensity of that particular command told Uhura how much he meant it. "Lieutenant Palmer, are we receiving any communications from the Shechenag ship?"

"I'm not sure, sir." Palmer threw an urgent glance, not at Spock but at Uhura. "There's *something* coming in past the subspace interference, but I've run it through every one of our translating algorithms and it still doesn't turn into language."

"That's because we didn't have working universal translators when the Shechenag spoke to us down on Tlaoli. They translated their language for us." Uhura crossed the bridge toward the communications station without waiting for an order from Spock. As the senior communications officer on the *Enterprise,* it was her prerogative to replace a junior officer in times of crisis. And judging from Palmer's grateful look as she vacated the station, this qualified as one of those times.

Uhura located the channel Palmer had been monitoring, full of the clattering mechanical sounds of

Shechenag speech, and routed it to the ship's neurolinguistic analyzing circuits instead of through the communications station's simpler bank of preprogrammed translation routines. Unfortunately, even the powerful ship's computer would take several minutes to begin breaking down the structure and vocabulary of the alien language, especially if parts of it were actually machine control code as Uhura suspected from the sound. By the time the *Enterprise* crew figured out what the Shechenag were trying to tell them, the two ships might well be engaged in a totally unnecessary battle.

Uhura took a deep breath and adjusted her transmitter to the same frequency the Shechenag were using, then glanced at Spock. "Request permission to reply to the Shechenag, Commander."

"Granted."

Uhura opened a channel back to the alien ship, hoping the muffled sound of machine noise in the background meant that it was being monitored. "This is not the language," she said firmly, trying to replicate as best she could the flat declarative sentence structure of the cybernetic aliens. "We do not intend hostility. We do not understand your orders."

The rattles and whistles on the translator channel stopped abruptly. A moment later, much to Uhura's relief, the shadowy silhouette of the alien ship slowed to a menacing hover on the viewscreen—much too close for comfort, she thought, but at least no longer advancing. She could tell from the almost dazed expressions of relief on the faces of Rhada and DePaul that there hadn't been much room left to maneuver between the two ships. Uhura suspected that even Kirk, with his steel nerves and fierce determination, might not have been able to watch another ship so nearly collide with his own and not have ordered an attack.

A light flashed on Uhura's board, and she felt her own tension melt a little. "The Shechenag are hailing us in English now, Mr. Spock. They're sending a visual signal as well."

"Put it on the main screen, Lieutenant." If Spock was at all shaken by the near miss they'd just barely avoided, neither his measured voice nor his erect posture showed it. He remained standing by Giotto at the security station, although Uhura couldn't tell if that was because he didn't trust the security chief or because he didn't think a race as alien as the Shechenag would know or care who occupied the captain's chair on the *Enterprise.*

"This is the language." The visual signal from the other ship showed a knot of dark metallic bodies, each with several spidery appendages extended to plug into oddly barren panels around the small bridge of their ship. Uhura couldn't see the torso tanks where the actual aliens were housed, and realized that they must be facing each other at the center of that mechanical huddle. Information from their ship systems and communications must be routed directly to their internal visual displays and control panels,

Uhura thought, but apparently they had encountered enough other species to recognize that external viewscreens existed.

"This is the language," she confirmed, seeing Spock nod at her to continue the conversation. "Please repeat previous communications."

"This is not the position."

Only silence followed that enigmatic statement. Uhura wondered if the Shechenag truly thought in such vague and abstract modes, or if their translating technology simply wasn't very good at conveying their true meaning in English. She tapped in a silent query to the ship's computer to see how much progress it had made on decoding the clattering alien speech, but the bar showing its progress had barely crawled a third of the way toward completion.

Spock glanced at her with a lifted eyebrow and Uhura turned her hands up, silently conveying her inability to interpret the Shechenag response. The Vulcan stared at the screen for a moment, then said with just a hint of question in his voice, "The correct position is farther away from the planet."

"Correct position is outside the planetary system." Despite the flat mechanical quality of the Shechenag's translated speech, Uhura had a feeling that statement might have originally held something close to sarcasm. "Eight hours remain allotted for permanent relocation." Several mechanical appendages rose and fell out of the clotted group of Shechenag who seemed to be jointly in command of their ship, as if to emphasize the next point. "Temporary relocation to higher orbital level must be effected immediately. Maintenance of current position will result in irreparable damage."

Spock turned away from the viewscreen's automatic visual pickup, so that all the Shechenag could see was the back of his dark head.

"Lieutenant Uhura, can you degrade our audio signal without actually terminating contact? Lift your hand to your face or turn away from the viewscreen before you answer, please."

Uhura swung around and dropped her gaze to her controls, as if some alarm there had caught her attention. Although she was more used to clearing communication channels than deliberately obscuring them, it took her only a few seconds to broaden the frequency range on their transmission to the Shechenag until it overlapped and included one of Tlaoli's screeching zones of subspace interference. "Done, sir."

"Very good. I wish to know why the Shechenag think our current orbit will cause us damage. Are we experiencing any difficulties in maintaining orbit, Mr. Rhada?"

The pilot coughed, then kept one hand balled at her mouth, as if to stifle further outbursts. "No, sir," she said behind that shield. "No more than the usual instability we've gotten from Tlaoli's gravitational shifts. We're down at the low end of the safe orbital range, but we should be able to maintain here indefinitely."

Spock nodded without turning around. "Mr. Washburn, what about the ship's power supplies? Any sign of problems?"

"No, sir." The engineer's shoulders stiffened, as if he had to actively fight the urge to turn and face his superior officer as he reported. "Mr. Scott says our warp core and engines are fully functioning again, and he's got a backup power supply isolated behind magnetic shielding, in case we suffer another ship-wide power drain."

From the science desk, astrobiologist Ann Mulhall cleared her throat. "Permission to make an observation, Commander?" she asked without turning around to look at the Vulcan.

"Granted, Dr. Mulhall."

"From what I have observed of Shechenag vocal structures, they are not as straightforward as their simple grammar and lack of dependent clauses may make them appear. They actually seem to contain a great deal of deliberate ambiguity, or even tactical misrepresentation."

"You mean the Shechenag are lying to us?" Uhura asked behind the cover of raising her frequency monitor to her ear.

Mulhall shook her head. "Not lying, necessarily, just not telling us a very understandable version of the truth. For instance, the irreparable damage they mention might refer to their ship rather than to ours."

"Or," said Spock with slowly lifting eyebrows, "to

the defensive satellite network they are installing around Tlaoli?"

"Quite possibly," agreed the astrobiologist.

"Thank you, Lieutenant Commander, for that insight." The Vulcan's angular face was suddenly very thoughtful. "Mr. Giotto, cancel the red alert. Mr. Rhada, prepare to lay in an orbit at the high end of the stable range, at least another thousand kilometers farther out from the planet. Lieutenant Uhura, slowly fade the interference out of our channel to the Shechenag and re-establish audio contact." The flurry of orders came so quickly that, for a moment, Uhura almost felt as if Captain Kirk were back in command of the *Enterprise.* The impression was deepened by Spock's next words, spoken into the communications panel on the captain's chair. "All senior officers report to the main briefing room. We have a battle plan to construct."

The knock on Sulu's cabin door was so tentative it barely woke him, even from an uneasy and drifting sleep. He lifted his head from his pillow, wondering if he'd heard a thump from some crewman passing in the corridor outside, but after a moment the quiet knocking sounded again.

"Come in." Since he'd lain down in his uniform, all Sulu had to do now was swing his feet off the bed and scrub the remnants of sleep from his face. The catnap hadn't done much to drive away the lingering jitters from his trip through the Janus Gate. Dr. McCoy had spoken soothingly about the natural adrenaline rebound effects after a period of suppressing strong emotions like panic and despair, but Sulu still wondered if the alien healing chamber had done something permanent to him. He had thought about asking the older version of himself if he felt anything similar after he'd come through the Gate, but an unaccountable shyness had walked Sulu past the other man and out of sickbay without making a conscious decision to put off any direct conversation.

The cabin door slid open, and a young gold-clad ensign edged just far enough inside that the door's automatic sensor wouldn't order it to shut again. "You're needed in the main briefing room, sir."

The somber dark eyes would have told Sulu who he was even if the Russian accent hadn't, but the rest of this younger Chekov's face seemed strangely unfamiliar. It wasn't the lack of scarring, Sulu decided, because he'd had time in the alien cavern and the shuttle to get used to the older Chekov's healed face. No, it was something completely different about their expressions, something even more fundamental than the shared line of their eyebrows or curve of their jaw...

Chekov shifted from foot to foot, reddening self-consciously beneath Sulu's intent gaze, but all he did was ask very politely, "Sir, did you hear me?"

"Yes. Sorry." Sulu stamped his feet into his boots and stood, glancing over at the communications console near his room's computer port. No message lights were flashing there. "Why didn't Commander Spock just hail me?"

Chekov gave him a startled look, as if he couldn't believe a senior officer was really asking him for information. "Um...I think he didn't want there to be any confusion, sir. About which version of us was supposed to come to the briefing, I mean."

"So you were summoned, too?" Sulu fell into step beside him as they exited the cabin and headed for the turbolifts. After spending hours on Basaraba with the brusque older version of Chekov, he couldn't resist the chance to find out how different this young Russian was from the man the Gorn invasion had turned him into. "Does that mean we're going back down to the planet?"

"I think so, sir." So far, Chekov seemed a lot like any other brand-new ensign fresh from the Academy—a little shy but not so reserved that he couldn't be drawn into a friendly conversation. "I heard Mr. Sanner and Lieutenant Tomlinson get called to this meeting, too, while I was on my way to get you."

"But not our...er...other halves?"

Chekov shot him another sidelong look as they stepped into the turbolift. "I guess not," was all he said, but there was a more relaxed tone to his voice now, as if Sulu's tacit admission of discomfort about having an older doppelganger aboard ship had eased a little of his own awkwardness. "Mr. Spock didn't request Captain Kirk's younger self, either. I had to find someone else to keep an eye on him for a while." The Russian blew out an exasperated breath. "He refused to go to sleep as the doctor ordered. I not only had to show him every public area on the ship, I had to haul him out of just about every maintenance shaft, too!"

Chekov sounded so much like an indignant older brother that Sulu couldn't help laughing. "Well, what did you expect? He *is* going to grow up to be the captain. What did you end up doing with him?"

The young ensign flashed him a surprisingly mischievous glance. "I gave him to the captain's yeoman. I told him she might let him see the captain's quarters if he promised to behave himself."

Before Sulu could reply, the turbolift doors slid open on the corridor leading to the ship's main briefing room. Another turbolift opened across the passage and Sulu suddenly felt as if he was gazing into a mirror. The older versions of Sulu and Chekov looked back at them steadily, although there was a twinkle in one pair of dark eyes that wasn't matched in the other.

"Heading for the briefing?" the older Asian man inquired as he stepped out into the hallway.

"Uh...yes." Sulu had to push Chekov forward out of the opening so the turbolift doors could close. The young ensign's face had stiffened into self-consciousness again. "Were you called in, too?" He put as much innocence as he could muster into that question, but his older self apparently knew all the tones of his own voice too well to be deceived. He gave Sulu an ironic glance as they continued down the corridor. The older and younger Russians followed behind in stony silence.

"Not specifically," the older Sulu said. "But seeing that we have about half a century of Starfleet experience between us, we thought we qualified as senior officers."

The briefing room doors slid open to reveal a room already full of crewmen: Scotty, Giotto, McCoy, and Uhura in addition to Commander Spock. Lieutenant Robert Tomlinson and Zap Sanner stood quietly at the back, leaving the last empty chair at the table for an officer with a higher rank than theirs. Sulu tapped the younger Chekov on the shoulder and started around the room to join them, but was stopped by the sound of Spock's austerely cleared throat.

"Did you misunderstand my orders, Ensign Chekov?"

Sulu could see the ensign stiffen into the rigid heads-up posture Starfleet cadets were taught to assume when being disciplined for an infraction of academy rules. "No, sir," was all he said. Sulu opened his mouth to defend him, but his older self stepped forward and motioned him to silence.

"We heard you call a senior officer's briefing to draw up a battle plan, Mr. Spock," said the older Sulu. "It seemed like something we might be able to help with."

"I am not certain Starfleet regulations permit you to take part in this planning session, Captain Sulu. You are not currently a line officer on this ship."

"But visiting captains have consultation privileges," the older man reminded him. "And in my experience, no one objected if they brought their executive officers along. Of course, we had a lot more actual battle planning sessions in our future than you ever had in your past."

The subtle hint didn't change Spock's expression, but Sulu saw Chief Engineer Scott rub thoughtfully at his chin. "You may as well let them be, Mr. Spock," he suggested. "Otherwise, we'll just be explaining the whole thing over again to them when we're done."

The older Chekov stirred and spoke for the first time since emerging from the turbolifts. "If we're going to be part of your battle plan, then we're definitely staying." He took a step over to the empty chair and clenched his hands upon its back, as if to claim it for his superior officer. "So, what do you want us to do?"

A tinge of asperity crept into Spock's voice, although his angular face never changed expression. "The situation is not quite that simple, Commander Chekov. You should be aware that if we succeed in retrieving Captain Kirk from the past and restoring the timeline that he should have created, your own existence—"

"—will pop and disappear like a soap bubble?" The Russian exchanged ironic glances with his captain as he swung the chair around for the older Sulu to sit. "We're aware of that, Mr. Spock."

"Then I presume you understand why I cannot allow you to consult with us now." Spock lifted an eyebrow at the questioning looks the older men gave him. "Logically, neither you nor Captain Sulu may be considered to be allies in any attempt we make to repair the timeline that is keeping you alive."

It was the shoes that reminded him. A stupid little detail that hadn't troubled his mind in nearly nineteen years, the shoes littering the streets around the Federation embassy struck Captain James Kirk now as a poignant indictment of just how helpless they'd all been that night.

"Damned cowards," his father had complained at the time as he hurried his wife and sons past the embassy's public reception area and through the mysterious door stamped STARFLEET PERSONNEL ONLY. Being only fourteen, Kirk had been forced to lever himself up on tiptoe using his brother Sam's shoulder in order to catch a glimpse of what had most recently inspired his father's disgust. Outside the big unbreakable front window, the embassy's native personnel were stripping off their clothes as they ran.

A firm hand had splayed between his shoulder blades, gentle despite the tension Kirk could feel in the press of its fingers, and he let his mother hurry him forward without objecting. Somewhere behind them, he could hear urgent voices conferring over communicator channels, but couldn't quite make out what they were saying.

"They're frightened," his mother said. He knew she was trying to sound collected and brave for him and Sam, but she succeeded in only sounding fearfully close to tears. "They've been working in conjunction with Starfleet, and now they're afraid of what's going to happen to them and their families."

"Fourteen months we've spent working with them," George Kirk agreed bitterly, as usual only hearing the words spoken and not what his wife was trying to say. "Fourteen months, and the minute things go south, they're stripping out of their uniforms and leaving us to cover their retreat."

"George, that's not fair..."

A flutter of cloth blew up against Captain James Kirk's chest now, and he snatched at it with the hand not encumbered by the gauss rifle. What a few hours ago had been a neat blue-and-silver tunic flapped spastically in the breeze, half the buttons now ripped from its placard and the grimy outline of a bare Grexxen foot stamped across its back. Kirk felt a strange whirl of vertigo as he rubbed the soft cloth between his fingers, expecting to find it half-rotted and weather-torn. It didn't feel right to be coming across this fresh evidence of the Federation's failure here. It had all been so long ago...but somehow, this long-ago battle had been turned into the reality of here and now.

Up ahead of him, George Kirk lifted a hand to signal *wait* before creeping up the embankment that marked the edge of the wide boulevard the Grexxen called Ith. Roads in Sogo—and elsewhere on Grex, Kirk had always assumed—were evolutionary end products of the organic, looping footpaths Kozhu and Vragax had made over the generations. They had names the way humans named pets, not arbitrary appellations that could be changed with each swing of the political climate. Ith was not Ith Street, or Ith Avenue, it was only Ith and it would remain Ith until the last Grexxen passed away.

A fate the Vragax seemed determined to hasten on this particular evening.

Kirk joined his father on the slope of the embankment when George waved him forward, rolling to his back so he could keep watch behind them while George lifted up to scout ahead. "The fighting's moved farther south," Kirk whispered, taking the moment of stillness to thumb the last of his shells into the gauss rifle and toss the empty magazine away.

George grunted wordlessly in reply.

"That means there's a good chance your son made it back to the embassy all right."

Another grunt, this one carrying a wealth of skepticism. "I just hope he had the sense to head there."

Kirk kept his face turned toward the firelit streets behind them. Part of him wanted to tell his father that he was being unfair to his son, but he knew himself well enough to realize that was just a ghost of adolescent indignation. *You really couldn't blame George Kirk for feeling that way,* he thought, a little surprised by the embarrassment that stirred, ever so faintly, in the pit of his stomach. It wasn't like his younger self hadn't given his father every reason to distrust him this night nineteen years ago—it was just hard to separate where things had started from where they ended up when the excitement was all over.

The last time George Kirk had seen his youngest son on Grex, the boy was wedged into a narrow corridor alongside his mother and older brother, trying very hard not to seem as frightened as he'd become during their hurried evacuation of the staff apartments. He and Sam were the only children, his mother the only woman not clutching an attaché of vital Federation documents or brandishing a phaser.

"Stay with Ensign McCullough." George Kirk held his wife by the shoulders and looked sternly into her eyes, apparently convinced that she wouldn't understand these simple instructions unless she was looking straight at him. "She'll take care of you and the boys until I can join you on the *Eliza Mae.*"

His mother nodded dutifully, but her dark eyes were wide and uncomprehending. "How will we know where to find you? What if the *Eliza Mae* can't pick up everyone? What will happen then?" It bothered Kirk more than he liked to admit, hearing his mother sound so much like a frightened girl.

In one of his rare moments of tenderness, George Kirk reached up to gently sweep her hair aside and cup his hand to the side of her face. "You don't have to find me," he promised softly. "The *Eliza Mae* will have room for everybody, and I'll be coming right behind you, just as soon as all the noncombatants are clear." He kissed her quickly and with an uncharacteristic lack of reserve. "You look after the boys. I can take care of myself." Then he looked a question Kirk didn't understand over her shoulder at the stocky blond security guard, and McCullough nodded once, curtly, in reply. Apparently satisfied with that answer, George stepped back from his wife and summoned the small team of men waiting for him with a wave of his arm. They disappeared down the hall toward the embassy proper without even a backward glance.

"If you'll come with me, Mrs. Kirk." McCullough took her arm before Kirk's mother had a chance to answer, drawing her away from the embassy with resolute politeness. "We'll all be out of here soon, but we have to keep moving."

They had packed in behind the rest of the evacuees, herded down the narrow hallway like sheep through shearing gates. But instead of clever dogs, what pushed them along were the screams that had started up on the streets outside, and the reflections of fires on the walls of the rooms they left behind. Kirk shuffled along with everyone else, clinging to Sam's belt to keep from being separated in all the pushing and confusion. By the time they reached the outside, he was overhot and breathing hard, and the lack of a cool night breeze only made him feel dizzy and sick. Instead of the refreshing autumn bite he'd grown to expect from Grexxen evenings, the air was hot and dry with heat blown over the walls from the fires outside. Flakes of ash drifted down like tiny leaves from monochromatic trees. Kirk watched a small Work Bee vehicle make a swift vertical ascent from the embassy's shuttlepad, its belly painted amber by the burning city streets below it.

His mother combed hair back from her face with one hand and craned her neck to watch the Work Bee disappear. Another small craft almost immediately took its place. "What if they shoot us down before we get out of atmosphere?" she asked McCullough fearfully.

"They can't, ma'am. They've only got projectile weapons and a few phasers, nothing that can hurt the spacecraft once we're airborne." To this day, Kirk didn't know if McCullough honestly believed that was true, or if she'd only said it to comfort the wife of her commander.

They crossed the short expanse of open tarmac at a run, and McCullough sprinted ahead of them to hold the hatch open with her body and push them all in ahead of her. The inside of the tiny maintenance shuttle stank of sweat and panic, crammed almost to bursting with panting bureaucrats and administrators. The seats had been removed, along with all the tools and equipment the shuttle usually carried, and Kirk wondered for one awful moment whether or not this was actually a ship that was supposed to go outside an atmosphere. Thinking back on it now, he realized that this was the moment when he became truly afraid, the point at which he understood that things on Grex had gotten so bad that they would never be fixed and the people crowded into this shuttle alongside him were actually fleeing for their lives.

Just as that realization rocked him, he heard the frantic cry from outside. "Wait!"

The men who had been hauling shut the hatch hesitated, and another young man came running up to shoulder his way inside. His face was flushed, his neat business suit ash-stained and rumpled. But, unlike the other embassy staffers, instead of an overstuffed briefcase he hugged two young children in his arms. The older of the two whimpered fitfully, her face buried against his shoulder as though she couldn't be frightened by what she couldn't see; the younger one stared about the crowded shuttle with huge copper eyes, her round, bronze face angelic with fascination.

Behind Kirk, McCullough announced, not unkindly, "You can't bring them with you, sir."

The young man stared at her. For some reason, Kirk noticed that his eyes were startlingly blue. "You can't expect me to leave them." His British accent seemed perversely civilized and out of place amid all the violence.

"There isn't room, sir—"

"But they're Kozhu!"

"It doesn't matter."

"Their mother gave them to me." He cast pleading eyes around the shuttle. "She was one of the interim adjudicators. The Vragax all know who she is! They'll kill her—they'll kill her family!" He squeezed the children tighter, turning half away from McCullough as though daring her to try and take them. "Please, they're only children…"

McCullough was silent for a long, painful moment, and the Starfleet pilot at the front of the craft called back, "It doesn't matter who or what they are. We're overweight as it is. We might still make it into orbit with you on board, but with you and both the kids..." He shook his head ruefully. "I'm sorry."

*They're small,* Kirk thought with almost analytical clarity. *They don't even have to stand on the floor.* He ducked under Sam's arm and past the men at the hatch without consciously thinking about what he intended. But by the time his feet hit the tarmac, he was giddy with the rightness of what he was doing.

"Jimmy!" He heard a commotion inside the shuttle that he assumed was his mother lunging forward after him and McCullough and Sam restraining her. "James Tiberius Kirk, you get back inside this shuttle *this minute!"*

He backed away from the hatchway, just in case she proved able to shrug McCullough off. "Mom, it's okay! I'll take the next transport!" *I'm George Kirk's son—they're not going to leave me behind.* He wasn't so sure about two alien toddlers. "You go on. I'll be fine!"

"We haven't got time for this," the pilot complained from the front of the shuttle, and Kirk yelled back, "Take off without me! I'm okay!" before his mother could order him aboard again.

Just then, a big hand clamped on the back of his neck and pulled him another two steps back from the open hatchway. "I've got him, Rivas." Lieutenant

John Maione tucked Kirk against another of the guards behind him with only a token thump of his hand against the boy's chest as a reprimand. "Go ahead and lift off. Jimmy can ride out with us. I'll make sure the chief knows." Until that moment, Kirk hadn't realized that he and his mother and brother had been packed aboard the very last shipload of civilians on Grex—if Maione and his commandos were lining up to board the next vehicle, that meant there was no one else left to evacuate. The thought of riding into orbit with the embassy's elite protection troops filled young Kirk with a giddy excitement.

The shuttle's thrusters roared up to power, and brittle leaves skated away from the outtakes just as someone inside leaned out to haul the hatchway closed. "Thanks, John." Rivas's voice only just beat the booming of the shuttle's door. "Take care."

Maione shooed Kirk away from the pad to make room for the next vessel's landing, but the look on his face was wry with amusement, not the anger Kirk expected. "You're dad's gonna kill you." The lieutenant swiped away dry leaves that had clung to the boy's curly hair. "You know, Jim, you might want to save some of that nobility until you're a little older."

Later, when his father railed at him for being self-centered, thoughtless, and irresponsible, he clung to the word *nobility* with all the strength of his young heart.

But both his youthful nobility and its consequences were years in the past now. Or at least several hours. Captain James Kirk realized, as he watched his father click shut a portable IR scanner that he must have found among Maione's men, that he didn't even know what had ever become of the softhearted Englishman and his two young native wards. He remembered that the *Eliza Mae* had arrived only seventeen hours after the evacuation, and that none of the impromptu lifeboats had suffered losses during that time, but he had no idea where anyone who had fled with them ended up after that night. He resolved to seek the young Englishman out just as soon as he was back in his proper time frame.

"All clear." George tucked the IR scanner into his belt and clambered on hands and knees up to the surface of Ith. Even the building fires were dimming by now, their automatic fire suppression systems kicking in despite the chaos running rampant through the streets around them. Kirk and his father covered the last few blocks to the embassy without seeing any sign of the natives they'd be leaving behind. Except for the empty shoes.

The last Federation-owned ship on the planet was an all-but-disposable cargo sloop which had come through the atmosphere when the embassy crew first arrived and really wasn't expected to leave it again. Technically it had boosters enough to put it back into orbit in the event its initial cargo delivery had to be aborted for some reason. Technically. Kirk had never actually heard of anyone attempting such a feat before.

A tall figure, so thin it might have been built entirely of sticks, peeled away from the cargo sloop's shadow and came partway to meet them. "Did you not find him, Chief? Or has he just grown quite a bit from this morning?"

Kirk recognized the melodious voice as belonging to Arran Mutawbe, George Kirk's second-in-command. Even after all these years, he remembered Mutawbe's fierce, ready smile and gentle sense of humor as clearly as he remembered the man's beautiful voice. For some reason, though, he hadn't recalled that Mutawbe stood well over two meters tall. Maybe it was because everyone was taller than he was when he was fourteen, and his young mind hadn't made a distinction based on how much taller they were.

"This is Captain Forester from the last personnel drop." George's voice was as curt and steady as always, but Kirk noticed that he stepped up his pace to the shuttle without waiting to see if Kirk and Mutawbe followed. "Jimmy's not here?"

"No, sir. But we've been hard-pressed to keep a good lookout—the rebels keep circling back to snipe at us. Rory thinks he saw a couple of Starfleet boys near the tree line a little while ago, but we're not missing anybody and I don't trust the Vragax not to be luring us out into the open." Mutawbe took the gauss rifle when George handed it to him, then the IR scanner and the shock grenades. "Tony took one in the face last time the snipers was past, sir." His voice lowered sadly. "He's not doing so good."

George threw additional equipment off his utility belt into the floor of the sloop, then began reaching in to pull out a fresh phaser and a heavy shoulder bag that Kirk realized with a start was an antique tricorder.

*No, not antique—probably brand new.*

"Then you've got to get Tony out of here," George said without turning around. He tucked the phaser into his belt, then pulled out a communicator and flipped it open to run a check of its circuits.

Mutawbe watched his commander for a moment, then asked carefully, "What about your boy, sir?"

George picked up a handful of extra power supplies for both the phaser and the tricorder, fitting them one by one into his rapidly filling belt. "I'll find him."

"And we'll wait, sir—"

George spun on Mutawbe, his expression in the waning firelight desperate and fierce. "No, you will not wait." He wrestled his tone back under control before continuing. "I will not put any more of my men at risk because my son ran off on some half-cocked adventure. You'll get in this sloop and take Tony and the others into orbit where they'll be safe until *Eliza Mae* arrives. She's three days out, tops. If I can't find Jimmy by then…"

He fell silent, but Kirk knew what he was thinking. *If I can't find him by then, he's nowhere here to be found.* The trouble was, Kirk had a feeling that was already true.

# Chapter Five

THE MAIN BRIEFING ROOM on the *Enterprise* froze into silence, the crystalline kind of silence Uhura usually associated with the instant just before a photon bomb went off. Then the older version of Chekov startled her, not by exploding but by wheeling to fix the younger version of Sulu with an unblinking stare.

"*You* saw our future," he said. "How certain are you that I would die to prevent it from happening?"

Sulu looked from the older man to Mr. Spock. "Completely," was all he said, but his voice carried a wealth of conviction. From across the table, McCoy gave Uhura a speaking glance and jerked his head toward the older version of Sulu.

"And we know Captain Sulu would do that, too,"

Uhura said. "If it weren't for the Janus Gate, he would already have died to stop the Gorn invasion."

"I am aware of that, Lieutenant," Spock said crisply. "But Captain Sulu's loyalty to his own timeline does not imply an equal willingness to sacrifice himself for ours."

The older starship captain smiled. "I had forgotten what a stickler you were for logical certainty, Mr. Spock. I don't know if I can give you any guarantee that Chekov and I are committed to helping you restore the timeline that has your lost Captain Kirk in it. But if we look at this logically...Right now we're floating in an isolated time bubble you created when you cold-started the engines back at Psi 2000. Is that right?"

"That is correct." Spock's voice had taken on an edge it held so rarely that it took Uhura a moment to recognize it as impatience. "We have only twenty-eight hours of that time bubble left before we rejoin the main timestream and once again become the only *Enterprise* in the galaxy. At that point, I calculate a ninety-seven percent probability that we will no longer remember Captain Kirk, and thus will lose all hope of repairing the damage we have done to the past."

Sulu nodded. "And if that happens, if we don't manage to repair the timeline by that point, what will happen to me and Chekov?"

Spock lifted one eyebrow, as if the question was so meaningless it had never occurred him. Uhura cleared her throat as the silence lengthened.

"If the timeline we rejoin is the one that never had

a Captain Kirk in it," she hazarded, "then we might never have found this planet or left any survey teams here to discover the Janus Gate."

"And we definitely wouldn't have gotten thrown back in time," Zap Sanner chimed in. "Because, according to these guys, their *Enterprise* got to Psi 2000 too late to catch the virus that killed the research team there."

The older Sulu nodded, as if they'd confirmed what he was already thinking. "So if we don't repair the timeline and you never find or use the Janus Gate—"

"—then we won't be able to save you or Chekov from Basaraba." McCoy waggled a finger at Spock, looking gleeful at having caught him in a logical lapse. "So much for your worries about them sabotaging our plans! They're going to disappear in twenty-eight hours whether they help us or not."

Uhura took a deep, dismayed breath when she saw where this line of logic was leading. "But if we don't use the Janus Gate, you'll never find out that the Gorn are holding a Metron prisoner in Tesseract Fortress."

"Much less be able to free him and stop the Gorn invasion of Vulcan," the older Sulu agreed. "All in all, I think that gives us several logical reasons to help you get your captain back."

There was a brief silence, broken by several forceful Russian words. Despite her passing knowledge of the language, the phrase wasn't familiar to Uhura, but she saw a startled shade of red touch Ensign

Chekov's cheeks as he glanced at his scowling older counterpart.

*"That's* what you can do with your logical reasons," the older Chekov growled, staring steadily across at Spock. "I swore an oath when I was commissioned as a Starfleet officer. Rescuing fellow Starfleet personnel from danger was one of the things I promised to do. It doesn't matter where I am in time, I'm still a Starfleet officer."

The Vulcan gave the two older men a speculative look. "May I assume you would be willing to travel backward in time another twenty years in order to ensure the timeline is repaired?"

"Yes," said the older Sulu and the older Chekov in one voice.

Spock paused a moment, then inclined his head in a grave nod. It was probably as close as he could come to an apology, Uhura thought, and it was certainly all the satisfaction he intended to give a still-grinning McCoy. The first officer resumed their interrupted planning session before the doctor could make any other comments on his logical lapse.

"We are agreed that we will ignore the Shechenag's ultimatum to leave the system," the Vulcan said. "We must send the young James Kirk back to his proper place and time, and to do that we must have access to the Janus Gate. However, I would prefer not to engage an unknown race in battle, as that would be time-consuming at best and catastrophic at worst. Even if the Shechenag have forsworn the practice of war, their technology appears to include enough powerful defensive mechanisms that any confrontation with them could prove deadly."

The older version of Sulu nodded. "So our first priority is to take back control of the Janus Gate in a way that won't put us in direct conflict with its guardians. How do you plan to do that?"

"I have a strategy which I believe will allow us to disable a large enough sector of their defensive shield to get a shuttle through to the planet," Spock said. "If we wait until the Shechenag are occupied with installing the section of network opposite the Janus Gate's location—"

"But they left a guard down in the caverns," the older Chekov said brusquely. "Won't they alert the mother ship when they see us?"

Spock lifted an austere eyebrow at the interruption. "*If* they see us."

"How could they not?" That puzzled question came from the younger version of Sulu, who, like the older Chekov, had entered the caverns only through the Janus Gate, and exited only through the main entrance above the alien time transporter. Uhura opened her mouth to answer him, but to her surprise the younger version of Chekov spoke before she could.

"There's a back entrance to the cave system," he said quietly. "One so small and hard to get through that the Shechenag may not even know it's there."

Geologist Zap Sanner reached over to give the ensign an approving thump on the shoulder. "Finally figured out why they needed *us* on this mission, huh? I hope you still remember the path back from the healing chamber to the Janus Gate. The big meltdown that happened when we brought Lieutenant Sulu back from Basaraba probably took the last of my cave reflectors off the walls."

"It did?" The young Russian looked suddenly uncertain, his gaze shifting from Sulu to Uhura to Spock. "But—but it wasn't *me* who mapped that part of the caves," he blurted at last. "It was the Chekov who went into the Janus Gate and replaced me at the waterfall—"

His older self gave him an incredulous look across the table and Chekov fell silent, an even darker and more mortified blush staining his face. Fortunately, Spock did not appear to notice the ensign's embarrassment.

"I have programmed Lieutenant Jaeger's reconstructed maps into my shielded tricorder," the Vulcan said calmly. "Your knowledge of the caverns will only be required to guide us past the sections Mr. Jaeger and Mr. Sanner could not reconstruct."

Zap Sanner snorted beneath his breath. "That means we're there to carry the equipment again," he muttered to Chekov in a not-very-discreet aside.

"Indeed," said Spock. "It seems only logical to assign that function to crewmen who have the most experience with Tlaoli's caverns. And with the Janus Gate itself," he added, his intelligent glance sweeping back toward Uhura.

She nodded her understanding of that. "What

about the Janus device itself, Mr. Spock? Won't the Shechenag still be guarding it, even if they don't see us coming through the back entrance of the cave?"

"That would be a logical assumption," Spock agreed. "However, I did not observe any magnetic shielding on the robotic devices the Shechenag previously used to threaten us. If our plan to deactivate the defensive shield succeeds, much of the power supply will already have been drained from those devices. We should be able to engage the remaining Shechenag in hand-to-hand combat."

"Why not just blast the whole damned cave with phaser fire from the ship, the way we did before?" McCoy demanded. "That would take all the guards out, and charge the gate up at the same time."

Spock's eyebrows lifted in an expression which, in a human, Uhura might almost have called pained. "You may not have been attending to the part of our discussion, Doctor, in which we mentioned our intentions to approach the planet undetected by the Shechenag," he said with crushing formality. "I do not believe blasting our phasers down through their defensive network will accomplish that goal."

McCoy grunted acknowledgment of that. "All right, let's say we get a shuttle down to the planet and manage to take out the Shechenag guards. What do we do then?"

Spock's eyebrows arched a little farther. "Doctor, I believe you are suffering from the same lack of sleep and nutrition that you were so concerned about in the rest of us. Surely you recall our discussion about using the Janus Gate to send our version of Captain Kirk back to his proper place and time—"

"Of course I recall it," McCoy countered, somewhat irritably. *"You're* the one who's forgetting something here, Spock. Didn't we establish with Captain Sulu that the Janus Gate won't exchange a weaker version of someone for a healthier version? Wouldn't that keep us from putting young Kirk into the machine and sending him anywhere unless the adult version of him gets hurt or even killed back in the past?"

"I did not forget that, Doctor," Spock said tartly. "Upon our return to the ship, I scanned the *Enterprise* crew database to determine if anyone else among the crew was stationed on Grex during the brief Starfleet mission there. Out of a crew of three hundred and twenty-six, I calculated that the probability of finding such a crewman was approximately point one five eight, more than high enough—"

"Don't tell me what the odds were, Spock," McCoy interrupted. "Just tell me if you found somebody!"

Security Chief Giotto cleared his throat, a little gruffly. "He found somebody," the older man said. "I served in the embassy protection force on Grex for fourteen months, right up until the natives went on a rampage and threw us off the planet. I was on the very last transport out, but I don't remember much about the evacuation. I got hit in the face by a projectile weapon a few hours before we left, and I didn't wake up until we were back at Starbase Five."

"A life-threatening experience which makes Chief Giotto an ideal candidate for the Janus Gate's viewing mode," Spock said in satisfaction. "If we utilize Lieutenant Commander Giotto to create a connection back to Grex, in the same manner in which we used Lieutenant Uhura to create a connection forward to Basaraba, we can engage the Janus Gate's associative transport and return our young James Kirk to his proper time, if not his proper place in it."

"You're going to throw that boy into the middle of a violent native uprising?" McCoy demanded. "How the hell do you expect him to survive that?"

"By providing him with protection." Spock steepled his fingers meditatively. "It will be necessary to seek volunteers among the crew who would be willing to go back in time to protect young Kirk. However, since we know that the Shechenag will strenuously resist our attempts to use the Janus Gate again, we must presume that our ability to use the device will be limited. It may not be possible to send crewmen to Grex, then wait to make certain they safely deliver the boy to his father before we are driven away from the machine. If it becomes necessary to strand anyone in the past, we would create exactly the overlapping time disruptions about which the Shechenag warned us."

"That's easy enough to fix," said the older version of Sulu. "Instead of *Enterprise* crewmen, you send me and Chekov back with this once-and-future captain of yours. Since we're not going to exist at all once you get your real captain back, it won't hurt the timeline to leave us there."

"That would be the logical solution to our dilemma," Spock agreed calmly. "However, until your existences come to an end when our time bubble collapses, Captain Sulu and Commander Chekov, you remain sapient beings with the right of self-determination. Are you willing to volunteer for this mission?"

"Well, Pavel?" Captain Sulu glanced over his shoulder at his own first officer, his lips curving in an odd, bittersweet smile. "It's a second chance at suicide. What do you say?"

There was no answering smile on his executive officer's rigid face, but something hard and cold seemed to have melted from the older Russian's voice, leaving a thin trickle of amusement behind it. "Sure. When do we leave?"

*This is so wrong,* Kirk thought as he jogged behind his father through the abandoned streets of Sogo. It wasn't the untrafficked roads and half-burned buildings that made his stomach clench, but the fact that he knew he had never seen them this way before—the fact that *nothing* he'd experienced tonight was like what he'd gone through before. *History is different, and I don't know by how much, or why.*

Kirk's memories of the night his family fled from the Grexxen civil war had faded very little over the years. He remembered all too clearly jumping out of the shuttle that would carry his mother and Sam into orbit because of some misguided sense of heroism. He remembered narrowly escaping his father's wrath by immediately reboarding another ship with John Maione and his team of peacekeepers. And he remembered that when the peacekeepers' shuttle had been shot down by the Vragax, Kirk had fled back toward the embassy as fast as he could possibly run, only to be cut off and hunted down in an abandoned office building by a small group of marauding natives. In the past as Kirk remembered it, his father had stormed in and saved him mere moments before he was put to death, then he and George had met Mutawbe and the others back at the auxiliary landing pad where they had successfully escaped into orbit and were rescued by the *Eliza Mae* a mere handful of hours later.

But so many things were already different. Kirk as an adult had not been with his father—those Vragax hadn't lived to leave the office building where they'd cornered their human prey. George Kirk was not left behind on Grex to fend for himself and possibly die.

"God, there's not a native for blocks." George frowned down at the clunky, shoulder-strung tricorder he had balanced against his stomach. Faint gray light from the tricorder's tiny readout illuminated an irritable expression Kirk was beginning to suspect was his father's default when uncertain or under stress.

For some reason, he'd never made that connection as a child. "What about a human?"

George made a little sound of frustration. "I've got something that might be human life-signs this way—" He gestured into the darkness ahead of them and off to the right, then looked in the direction he'd just indicated as if to match what he saw against what the instrument was telling him. "—but it flutters in and out, so I'm not really sure." He turned his fierce glower back down toward the tricorder, and Kirk realized with a strange nudge of affection that his father was embarrassed. "But I could be reading this wrong. I've only used one of these things a couple of times."

The admission unfolded a realization for Kirk that he probably should have made sooner in his life. What his father meant wasn't that tricorders were so new or exotic that he'd never been exposed to them—they were neither—but rather that they'd always been someone else's province. George Kirk had never been one of the breathless command hopefuls who bounced here and there throughout Starfleet ships and installations, learning a little bit about everything on their way up the ranks. He had only ever been a security and weapons expert, and that was all he had wanted to be. The science officers handled the tricorders; George Kirk handled the phasers. When Kirk was a boy, he'd interpreted his father's contentment with his position as a secret indication of cowardice, or at the very least a lack of ambition. He hadn't realized then what it really meant to be a starship commander, or how important it was to have dedicated men like George Kirk in the ranks to assist a commander in doing his job.

"I'm sure you're reading it correctly." Kirk looked around at the buildings and neat lawns surrounding them, already half-recognizing where they were. "It's not like Sogo is crawling with humans anymore. And that's back toward where the Kozhu women said they last saw...your boy." He nodded George down a cross street that cut more or less in the direction they needed to go. "If nothing else, that's as good a place as any to start."

By now, Kirk was fairly certain that no matter where they began their search, they weren't going to find the fourteen-year-old James Kirk. In addition to all the other changes the adult Kirk could already identify in the timeline, his mind kept going back to the Kozhu woman's description of the Vragax soldiers who fled the office building where Kirk remembered being rescued by his father nineteen years ago. In the past Kirk remembered, the Vragax didn't live to leave that building; in the version of events he was living through now, they had not only left, they'd fled in terror, praying to their gods for protection. No fourteen-year-old human boy had put that kind of fear in them.

But seeing a human boy vanish into thin air right in front of them might have.

It was the only explanation Kirk could think of that made any kind of sense. Whatever had transported Captain James T. Kirk back to Grex from Tlaoli must have spirited his younger self away at the same time.

Which was why George Kirk hadn't been able to find his son to rescue him, and why Arran Mutawbe and the others had left the planet without their boss on board. It was also why Kirk couldn't let George out of his sight, not even for an instant.

The fourteen-year-old Kirk hadn't died on Grex that night, and neither had his father. And if anything happened to George before the younger Kirk was returned, there would be no one on Grex to protect the boy, no one to guarantee he escaped off-planet. Kirk didn't want to think about what that would mean for him personally when he finally got back to his own future.

*Spock, you'd better be working fast.*

George had only voiced a token argument when Kirk insisted upon staying with him to look for his son. Kirk wanted to stay relatively close to where he'd arrived—to maximize his chances of being in the right place at the right time when Spock finally managed to reverse whatever had thrown him here. And his father might be stubborn but he was very far from stupid. Two of them had a much better chance of surviving long enough to find the boy in the first place.

They'd departed the embassy with a tricorder, two communicators, and phasers with fresh power supplies. They'd left the gauss rifles on the landing pad, along with the dead leaves and the blowing ash from the smoldering embassy. Kirk had let his father take the tricorder to disguise the fact that he hadn't a clue how to use the ancient thing. George Kirk's only plan had been to use the tricorder to locate what had to be the only remaining human life-sign on the planet other than their own, and then to keep his son safe and hidden until the *Eliza Mae* made communicator contact when she came into system. Mutawbe hadn't known whether or not the *Eliza Mae* had a ship-to-surface transporter, and Kirk didn't remember the subject having come up nineteen years ago. But even if the only thing they could manage was to send back down one of the evacuation craft after it had been emptied of its refugees, they should still be able to get George and his son off the planet. Assuming, of course, that George and his son and the good Captain Forester managed to stay alive that long.

"You never asked me why."

Kirk shook off his reverie, glad that the darkness would hide the blush tightening his cheeks. *I'm not going to be much help keeping us alive if I don't keep my mind on the present... or the past...* "I never had to ask. He's your son. You can't leave him behind."

George shook his head impatiently, paused, then adjusted his course to cut through a breezeway between two low-slung cottages. "No, I don't mean that." He played with the controls on the tricorder, but Kirk sensed it was only to give himself an excuse not to lift his gaze. "I mean why I brought them here to begin with. Why I'd drag my family halfway across the galaxy to some primitive hellhole where the natives still kill each other because of what gods their ancestors worshiped."

*You're right. I never asked.* Not now, and certainly

not when he was a child. It wasn't that Kirk hadn't noticed that his family seemed to be the only one condemned to spend Terran summers on whatever ship or station or strange little outpost George Kirk had been sent to that year. Kirk had always envied all those other unseen children of his father's colleagues, the kids who got to hang out and play baseball with their schoolmates during summer vacation—the kids who *got* a summer vacation, instead of leaving Earth's beautiful spring in time to show up for what was invariably their destination's midwinter. No matter how much his mother insisted it was a very small sacrifice they made for their father, all Kirk ever remembered was the excruciating boredom of three eternal months confined to the civilian areas of diplomatic posts that hadn't been designed with teenage boys in mind.

Nineteen years and one unexplained time-jump later, he knew something as a starship captain that he hadn't been able to see as a boy. There *were* no other families. The men who served with his father were barely more than boys themselves, still the sons of parents barely older than George, who wrote letters home to mothers instead of wives. At fourteen, anyone over the age of twenty had seemed impossibly mature and adult to Kirk. From the lofty age of thirty-three, he sometimes wondered what Starfleet was thinking when it sent such young boys out into the dangerous world.

"Don't blame yourself. Command told you it was

safe. The Kozhu and Vragax were both involved in peace negotiations, there hadn't been ethnic violence in Sogo since before the Orion occupation." It was the same thing Kirk would have said to any crewman, but it unwound a knot of old anger he hadn't consciously realized he'd been holding. "Besides, it was only for the summer."

George stopped abruptly, jerking a sideways look at Kirk that drew his eyebrows together into a mistrustful glower. "How did you know I'd only brought them in for three months?"

Alarm clenched a cold fist in the pit of Kirk's stomach, and he stared at his father without being sure how to respond. Of course Forester wouldn't know something like that. He'd only just arrived on Grex, as far as George Kirk knew, and he shouldn't have cared one way or the other how one of the security guards here had arranged his family's vacation.

*Should I tell him?* Kirk didn't know why he'd hidden his identity to begin with, except from the vague sense that he should have as little impact on past events as possible. But hadn't the changes already wrought in the last few hours negated any chance he had of extricating himself without leaving evidence he'd been here? He opened his mouth, not entirely sure what he intended to say.

The tricorder in George's hand chirruped sharply. Flipping back the cover, the older man scowled down at the little screen as though irritated that it had interrupted them. Then a look of almost smooth intensity washed all emotion off his face, and he reached to grab Kirk by the arm and drag him through a broken doorway into a building's dark interior.

Kirk followed his father's lead, crouching in the shadows off to one side of the door and squinting out into the nighttime. He heard the band of Vragax before he saw them. They made their way down the middle of the street in no particular hurry, talking and laughing in their native tongue so loudly that they struck cheerful echoes off the buildings around them. There were five of them, three carrying bags that looked like pillowcases stuffed with random items, the other two taking turns balancing a bottle of what was probably the native liquor on the ends of their rifles.

Kirk waited until they'd passed out of sight—but not out of hearing—farther down the street to whisper to his father, "You can apparently read that thing well enough after all."

"The proximity alarms are the easy part." He turned down the device's volume controls, then padded over to a window to watch the Vragax go. "They're not even pretending to keep a watch out for enemies."

Kirk stood and went to join him at the window. "They know Starfleet's gone, and the Kozhu are probably all in hiding by now."

They crept out a rear entrance, making more of an effort now to stay off the main thoroughfares and in the shadows of buildings and bushes. Vragax passed them twice more, raucous and relaxed, and Kirk eventually realized that they were all headed in roughly the same direction. Motioning George to follow, he skirted a row of market stalls and lowered himself into a maze of elaborate landscaping that had somehow escaped the night's violence. Dry branches and spent blossoms crackled under his hands and knees as he crawled to the edge of the planting.

The huge garden followed the edge of a pretty stone quadrangle, raised up to what would be Grexxen eye-level. Lying beneath the tangled planting, Kirk scanned the open area with a sense of growing dread. Tents and campfires and even little circles of tables and chairs littered the blue stone courtyard, augmented by atonal music from a half dozen different electrical devices. Kirk smelled the deliciously spiced roast *dondurma* that was his only fond memory of Grex, and watched a group of Vragax warriors jostling playfully to be first to scoop his share out of the fire. In surreal contrast, a string of Kozhu women were tied one to another around the base of a bubbling fountain that had probably been quite restful before today.

"They're coming from every direction." Kirk risked lifting up on his elbows to watch another loose collection of Vragax wander in between two of the tall office buildings. They were greeted with much hooting and applause. "It's like a gypsy camp...or a bivouac."

Beside him, George angled the tricorder toward the black glass pyramid that crouched just behind the string of captive women. "Whatever it is, those human life-signs we've been following are right in the middle of it."

Reporting to the bridge for the first time since he'd come back to the *Enterprise* felt much stranger than Sulu expected. It wasn't just the fact that he'd crossed so much space and time since he'd last sat at the starship's helm. He'd also never before manned the helm dressed in a formfitting gold suit made of nanowoven fibers. The caving gear wasn't uncomfortable, since it adjusted its thermal properties to allow for insulation or ventilation as needed for any environment, and he wasn't even the only one wearing it—Giotto and Spock were also dressed for immediate shuttle departure—but it still made Sulu feel conspicuous. Or maybe that feeling came from knowing there was an older version of himself standing on the back deck of the bridge, watching their maneuvers against the Shechenag with a critical forty-seven-year-old eye.

"Are you ready, Mr. Sulu?"

"Not quite, sir." Sulu didn't glance up from the automated course corrections he was inputting to his piloting console, but he could tell from the silence at the other end of the ship's helm that Spock had already finished programming his own station. The first officer had sent Navigations Officer DePaul to man the long-range sensors several minutes after he'd ordered Sulu to relieve Rhada at the helm, but Spock had already finished rerouting the ship's transporter controls from the engineering station to the navigations computer, where he could do the complex calculations that would be required for the maneuvers they were about to attempt. Montgomery Scott had made no protest when the Vulcan informed him he would be the one controlling the transporter beam. No one else had the mental acuity and swift physical reflexes required to handle the duty Spock had assigned to himself.

Sulu's task was simpler but no less challenging: he had to keep the ship hovering in an absolutely true position above the planet while the transporter beam was being used. Any deviation, Spock had warned him, would result in the kind of total power loss that had almost caused the *Enterprise* to crash on Tlaoli thirty-six hours ago. If they'd been in orbit around any other planet, Sulu would have programmed the ship's computer to fire the delicate microbursts of impulse power at precisely the right instant to cancel out the combined vectors of gravity and centrifugal force. But Tlaoli's unpredictable gravitational fluctuations meant that the task of holding several thousand tons of starship perfectly still in space fell to her human pilot. All Sulu could do in advance was input many possible engine firing sequences into the helm computer, so that he could activate any one with a single tap instead of a time-consuming series of keystrokes. He assigned a double-right thrust to his last open control, then glanced up at Spock. "Ready, sir."

Spock acknowledged with a nod but never took his

gaze from the main viewscreen ahead. Since they had pulled back to the more distant orbit requested by the Shechenag, the rust-red disk of Tlaoli no longer spilled off the edges of the screen. It shone against the stars like an antique copper coin, the alien defense system a spiderweb of glittering strands across its face. No dark shadow smudged across the stars around it—the Shechenag ship was on the far side of the planet, installing the last satellites for its planetary shield. Spock had used the ship's long-range sensors to make sure of that back in the briefing room, when they had finalized their strategy. Now all they had to do was hope the aliens would remain engaged long enough for them to put their plan into effect.

"Lieutenant DePaul, give me a bearing from the location of the Janus Gate on the planet to the nearest Shechenag satellite."

"Aye, sir." The navigations officer squinted down at the science display screen, which was calibrated for Vulcan eyesight. "Bearing three-four-three-point eight, two-one-nine-point-two mark eight. Transmitting to your data station now."

"Acknowledged." Spock's thin fingers flew across the navigations board as he calibrated the angle and intensity he would need to give the transporter beam. "Mr. Sulu, are we stabilized above the planet?"

"Aye, sir." Sulu had been carefully adjusting the impulse engines ever since he'd told the first officer he was ready, guessing that Spock would waste no time in commencing the operation. At any moment, the Shechenag might finish installing their satellite network, or circle the planet to check on the side they'd already completed. The *Enterprise* could not be caught doing something as suspicious as transporting absolutely nothing back and forth through the space around Tlaoli.

"Keep us steady," Spock reminded him. "Activating transporter beam now."

Unlike phasers, there was no way to see a transporter beam as it cut through space. For Sulu, that was a blessing. He could ignore the viewscreen above his head and pay attention just to the tiny fluctuations of his piloting curves. So far, all the adjustments he'd had to make had been minor and easy to input by hand. But he knew the pattern of Tlaoli's gravitational jerks and bumps. Any minute now, one should be coming...

A minute flash of blue and yellow appeared on his screen as the *Enterprise* felt the incipient tug of altered gravitational pull and began to drift off-station. Sulu felt one of the preprogrammed controls depress under his fingers before he was even conscious of selecting it, and only knew it was the right one when his orbital curves merged back into a perfect white arc. Maybe he should be grateful for whatever alien adjustments the Tlaoli healing chamber had done to his stress hormones after all, Sulu thought as he gazed in some amazement at his own hands.

"I believe our first attempt at satellite deactivation has been successful," Spock said. He glanced up from the helm toward the viewscreen. "Enlarge sector eighteen to twenty-nine, Mr. Scott."

"Aye, sir." The viewscreen swooped closer and lost most of its resolution as the chief engineer magnified that section of the defensive array. Tlaoli's subspace interference meant that long-range sensors were far more limited in their ability to re-create a distant image here than in other systems, but there was still enough clarity to see the glimmering iridescence of force-lines crisscrossing the planet's murky copper atmosphere. Sulu scanned the screen eagerly, and found the gap he was looking for near the very top. Between two barely visible glints of satellite, there no longer glittered a bright crackling strand of protection. By aiming the ship's transporter beam at the precise angle required to refract it off that energy field and toward the Janus Gate below, Spock had linked the subterranean energy-storage capacity of the ancient time transporter with the satellite's internal power generator. And just as it had done to the *Enterprise* thirty hours previously, the Janus Gate had sucked the satellite dry.

"It doesn't seem to have propagated any further down the network," Scotty commented from his station on the back deck of the bridge.

"Precisely as I suspected," Spock replied. "Each Shechenag satellite is responsible for creating only a single line of force. Therefore, the failure of one will not result in a complete failure of the network." He glanced back across at DePaul. "I am awaiting the vector to the next satellite, Mr. DePaul."

"Sorry, sir." The navigator peered down at his brightly lit display again. "Bearing three-four-five-point-three, two-one-seven-point-zero mark two. Transmitting to your data station now."

"Acknowledged. Steady as she goes, Lieutenant Sulu."

Easier said than done, Sulu thought. Tlaoli's unpredictable gravity field had chosen just that instant to bounce the *Enterprise* through a series of chaotic tremors, each of which had to be counteracted individually. The pilot concentrated on shutting out all extraneous noise from the bridge, all the distracting sounds of voices and machines and even the hum of his own data station. His world condensed down to two things: the position of the *Enterprise* in space on his helm display and the rapid-fire series of impulse engine firings necessary to keep that pristine white spot from splitting itself into unstable blue and amber echoes. His fingers continued to move without conscious thought, sometimes flying across the manual input controls, sometimes stabbing at one of his preprogrammed firing sequences. It felt like the worst kind of piloting exercise he'd had to endure in his Academy days, the kind where the flight simulator kept throwing problems at you faster and faster until it found the point where you failed.

But this time, there could be no failure point. One slip of the transporter beam off the energy lines of the Shechenag defensive screen, and the Janus Gate would suck power down from the *Enterprise* just as efficiently and ruthlessly as it took it from the alien satellite network. Sulu had to be just as ruthless in his concentration, jettisoning all of his normal attentiveness to the other operations on the bridge. He hunched over his screen, taking full advantage of the hair-trigger reactivity that the Tlaoli healing chamber had given him, accidentally or perhaps on purpose...

*"Lieutenant Sulu."*

The intensity of those words finally snapped the pilot's focus away from his helm display. "What's wrong?" he demanded, his gaze skating around the bridge in search of some power loss that he hadn't been able to prevent. All he saw were blinking lights and glowing screens, along with a circle of somewhat startled-looking faces. It took another minute before Sulu realized they were all staring at *him.* "What happened?"

Spock lifted an eyebrow at him from the other end of the ship's helm control. The Vulcan's face looked a little tired, but intellectual curiosity flickered brightly in his eyes. "We have deactivated a sufficient number of Shechenag satellites to create a gap through which the shuttle may pass. You no longer need to keep the ship on station."

"Oh." Sulu glanced down at the helm display and had to forcibly stop himself from punching at another control to drag its slight bluish tinge of drift back to solid white. He closed his eyes for a moment, then carefully tapped in the course parameters that would put the ship back into a normal circling orbit of

Tlaoli. "If you would call Mr. Rhada back to the helm, sir."

"I have already done so," Spock said gently. "And she is standing right behind you."

Sulu glanced over his shoulder and saw the second-shift pilot eyeing him with the same awed expression as the rest of the bridge crew. *That wasn't me,* he wanted to cry out as he left the helm and followed Spock and Giotto toward the turbolift. *That was something Tlaoli did to me to make me like its recycled soldiers!*

But when he stumbled a little with an unexpected surge of muscle weakness as he took a step up to the back deck of the bridge, Sulu felt himself caught and steadied by a familiar hand. He glanced up into his own dark eyes, framed with crow's-feet and weathered lines and filled with a wry look of recognition.

"I remember that," the older man said. "It's the aftereffect of piloting through too much of a life-and-death crisis. Don't worry, it goes away after a while."

Sulu paused to let his older self enter the turbolift first while he considered the implications of what the other man had said. If a version of Sulu from a timeline in which he'd never been healed by ancient alien technology knew exactly what he was feeling now—

Captain Sulu gave him an amused look as he stepped into the turbolift in stunned silence. "What's the matter?" he asked, then his eyes narrowed perceptively. "Didn't you already know how good a pilot you were?"

"Not really," Sulu admitted. "I never had to pilot a ship in a situation that critical before."

"I know." His older self met his gaze with a steadiness and resolve that Sulu could only hope to be capable of some day. "And with any luck, if we can rescue your Captain Kirk and put him back where he belongs, you'll never have to do it again."

# Chapter Six

KIRK LOOKED FROM the black glass pyramid to the nearly incomprehensible tricorder readout in his father's hands, then back again. *This is not someplace I ever went to.* Not that such details mattered anymore. They had already strayed so far from events as Kirk remembered them that he was skeptical about whether things could still be set right again.

On the quadrangle below, Vragax moved back and forth between their scattered little camps like sightseers at a bazaar, greeting fellow militants with much laughing and shouting and tossing about of weaponry. Firelight glinted off their tight copper braids, and Kirk thought he could smell the astringent bite of *phak* leaves, which he remembered the natives chewed as a sort of natural amphetamine. He wondered how much of the violence tonight had actually been inspired by a fervent hatred of the Kozhu and how much by the promise of copious amounts of *phak* for all the Vragax left standing afterward.

Tipping the tricorder screen back toward his father, Kirk waited for one of the chattering bands of Vragax to pass out of earshot before whispering, "Are you sure the readings originate inside *that* structure?" There were a half dozen other buildings surrounding the quadrangle, most of them much less inconveniently situated. Even if the Kozhu prisoners hadn't been tethered just outside the pyramid's main entrance, the whole building was set too far into the quadrangle to make a covert approach from the rear possible.

George swung the tricorder in as wide an arc as he could manage beneath their brushy cover, then pursed his lips around an unhappy frown. "It's got to be." He quietly closed the cover and tucked the tricorder behind him. "And the readings are a lot stronger now. There's three in there for sure, maybe four."

"Three?" For some reason, that bit of information made Kirk's heart thump with alarm. "I thought your son was alone."

"That's what I've been assuming." George pushed off with his elbows to wriggle backward out of the bushes, and Kirk ducked his own head out of the tangle of dead foliage to follow. The dry snap and crackle of their retreat seemed dangerously loud to his adrenaline-raw nerves. He held his breath until he'd disentangled himself from the edge of the quadrangle, as though stilling his breathing would somehow make their presence less obvious.

"Jimmy must have hooked up with someone else who couldn't make it back to the embassy in time." Kirk heard his father climb to his feet once the older man had cleared the landscaping, then felt George reach down and grab hold of his foot to guide him out of the last of it as well. "At least he's not out in this all by himself."

Standing, Kirk dragged George away from the garden and the gradually filling quadrangle beyond it. "Who could Jimmy possibly be with?" he hissed, unable to shake his unease. The doorway he snugged them both into was one of the few around them still intact, its sculpted overhang plunging the little alcove into heavy shadow. "What other humans are left on this planet besides you and me?"

He couldn't see George's face through the darkness, but the flicker of distant light in the older man's eyes as he glanced uncomfortably to one side was unmistakable. "Someone must have survived from Maione's team..."

"No one survived, Commander. No one." There wasn't much Kirk was still certain of, but that ugly detail hadn't changed.

"There were aid workers," George persisted. "Civilian aid workers."

"And most of them returned to the embassy when the fighting first broke out yesterday. You loaded them onto shuttles yourself, along with the embassy staff."

George's eyes flashed back to Kirk's face with fierce intensity. Kirk could almost imagine the angry glower fueling that stare. "Well, who do you think is in there with him?"

"I don't know," Kirk admitted with a sigh. "That's what bothers me." His eyes had adjusted somewhat to the deeper dark, and he silenced George's protest with an upraised hand. "I'm not saying we shouldn't try and bring them out of there. But don't forget those supposed Starfleet officers Mutawbe's men saw. If the Vragax are trying to lure us into something ugly, this would be how to do it."

The elder Kirk seemed to consider that reasoning, his fingers drumming an impatient rhythm on the case of the tricorder. Just when Kirk thought his father would erupt in frustration, George said, very quietly and evenly, "If there's any chance at all that humans are really trapped inside that building, though, we've got to try and bring them out. Even if my son *isn't* with them."

There was no rational protest he could make to that. Kirk wondered why he'd never noticed before that his father was such an intensely principled man. Maybe it was because the ongoing conflict between dedicated family man and loyal officer so often manifested itself as ill-temper. It occurred to him that all great conflicts between fathers and sons revolved around the fact that you couldn't truly appreciate an adult until you were one.

Kirk stepped away from the doorway only long enough to quickly get his bearings and verify that no Vragax had wandered into their cul-de-sac. "All right..." He motioned George to follow him around the corner of the building, away from the quad. "If we're going in, let's at least try to do it discreetly."

George made a skeptical noise as he paused to check the charge on his phaser. "I don't know how discreet you think we can be with these odds." He counted the power supplies on his belt, picked out the freshest one. "I can take out maybe four at a time with a wide-angle stun, if they're grouped close enough, but there have to be fifty Vragax out there." He flashed Kirk a surprisingly familiar half smile. "How fast can you run?"

"There's not going to be any running." Kirk kicked aside dead leaves and the remnants of what had surely been impressive flower plantings in a former life. His foot thumped against something harder than the rest of the detritus and he stooped to sweep it clean. "At least not if we do this right." Finding a rock too small for his purposes, he straightened and moved on.

"There's a sort of underground marketplace underneath this whole area," he told his father as he carefully kicked his way down the length of the garden. "There are entrances that lead down into it from most of the buildings surrounding that quadrangle. If we can find one of them, we should be able to make our way over to underneath where you're reading those life-signs, then come up from below."

Stuffing his phaser back onto his belt, George hurried forward to help Kirk heft a landscaping rock much larger than the one he'd found before. "How do you know this?" he asked. "I thought you said you'd only just got here."

Kirk stopped himself from saying, *Mom went there once to buy souvenirs,* and instead substituted, "Your son mentioned that his mother came here once. He pointed it out as we flew over." Nodding George back away from the rock, Kirk took the full weight of it in his arms just long enough to swing it like a pendulum toward a ground floor window. He turned his face down toward one shoulder as the window imploded with a magnificent crash.

George came carefully forward from where he'd retreated halfway into the street. "Well," he remarked dryly, "that was certainly in keeping with your suggestion that we be discreet."

Kirk couldn't help but throw his father a boyish grin. "Actually, it is. With all the looting going on tonight, the Vragax are less likely to investigate a breaking window than two men skulking through the landscaping at the edges of their camp."

They broke in the last jagged glass teeth using smaller decorative stones, then braced a branch from one of the flowering trees lengthwise down the window channel so they could lift themselves through the opening without embedding glass shards in their palms. Inside, the rock Kirk had lobbed through the window served as a neat step down to a carpeted office floor and a startling lack of sound. Except for the scattered glass and the incongruous lump of stone, everything else inside sat neatly undisturbed, as though the killing and burning outside were half a galaxy away. A plant with beautiful mottled leaves and a spray of delicate white flowers decorated the edge of an organically curving workspace. It bobbed gently in the night breeze let in through the broken window. Kirk felt weirdly as though he'd just climbed through a portal from hell back into the civilized world.

The hallways beyond the office door stretched out like the dark conduits on Tlaoli, lit only faintly by the starlight filtering through windows at either end. Kirk thought ahead to navigating the underground marketplace without even starlight to see by, and suddenly found himself missing Zap Sanner's carbide lamps.

"Here... What's this?"

The doorway George waved him toward wasn't the same sort as the others lining the hall. Swept into a simple arch, it opened onto a gently sloping path paved in smooth mosaic cobbles. It all looked iron gray in the dim light, but Kirk could imagine the intricate pastel patterns that must be inlaid in the floor and walls. It was the Grexxen eye for delicate color that had first lured his mother down into this native market. Now, on the first night of the alien civil war, Kirk could see just far enough beyond the entrance to tell that the tunnel widened as it wound down into the darkness, but could make out nothing of its beauty.

George put out an arm to block him when Kirk

stepped forward to lead the way down. "No, sir. You're the captain, you shouldn't be out front. We don't even know for sure that the Vragax aren't bivouacked down there, too."

For some reason, that simple but earnest objection made Kirk smile. "I appreciate your concern, Commander," he said, pushing George's arm back down to his side. "But if anyone here needs to be protected, it's you. I'm not exactly in a position to take care of a teenage boy without his father around to help me." He drew his own phaser and made sure it was set on stun. "Stay close to the wall, and close to me. If we're going to trip over something in the dark, let's at least not have it be each other."

The wall beneath Kirk's hand felt cool and silky, like enameled wood, and he traced the gradual curve with light fingers as it drifted eternally away from him, trending both around and down. He tried not to force his eyes to focus in the dark, but instead concentrated on keeping his gaze level in an effort to stave off the dizziness he knew was coming as soon as they left the last faint light behind. Even so, he caught himself clinging to the memory of illumination as it fell away behind them. If he wasn't very careful, imagined shadows lured trust away from his hands and feet, and vertigo crashed over him every time the wall led in a direction that felt strange to his eyes or the floor altered slope even slightly. When the cobblestones under his feet finally leveled out, the transition felt abrupt and wrong. His foot clapped loudly as it tried to step down lower than the surface that was there, and he stumbled forward several steps before George caught him by the back of his belt and hauled him vertical again.

Then they stood silent in the heavy blackness and waited for the turbulent shadows to settle.

"What does the tricorder say?" Kirk asked at last. His voice sounded harsh and uncivil in the quiet, but was swallowed too quickly by the dark to be offensive.

Behind him, George cracked the rotating panel that covered the tricorder's face and cued it back to life. The modest light from its readout chased back the worst of the shadows and lifted a little cloud of brightness between them. "There." George turned to follow the reading, like a pointer following his nose. "Down that way, about a hundred meters."

The whole little market seemed less sinister now that a tiny bit of light reached out into it. Darkness still hid the farthest walls and most of the details, but quaintly stained kiosks winked at them as they crept by, and the fresh kiss of jasmine-scented blossoms drifted out from a wheeled cart overflowing with the same flowers Kirk had seen on the desktop upstairs. Who would take care of them now that their merchant had either been chased out of the city or killed? The thought of all those beautiful plants, dead and rotting in the darkness, was just one more tragedy on a list that was already far too long.

Slowing beside a shop front that looked like both it and its charming window boxes should be set up on the streets above, George turned in a slow circle without lifting his eyes from the tricorder screen. Kirk pulled up alongside him, glancing down at the readout from habit, then scowling at his own annoyance when he remembered again that he couldn't read the unfamiliar device. "What have we got?"

"I think we're in range of that building." George craned a look up, then seemed to realize that he couldn't tell anything that way and bent back to his tricorder. "There are a lot of Grexxen life-signs in range, but they're all off that way—" He gestured toward what Kirk hoped was the center of the quad. "The human signs are pretty much directly overhead, except..." His human faith in his own senses betrayed him again, and he glanced back up at the out-of-sight ceiling with a grumble. "We're in the middle of everything down here. There may not be an entrance into that building."

Kirk looked up as well, but what he saw was at least a possibility. "Then I guess we'll just have to make one."

They moved the alien jasmine in armloads, settling the plants as gently as possible around the feet of a potted tree. The wagon itself turned out to be bolted into place. George freed it with two smartly placed shots from his phaser, then swore when Kirk laughed because they had to wait for their eyes to recover from the brilliance. Once under the human life-signs, they braced the wheels with the flower boxes from the little shop, and Kirk climbed unsteadily aboard while George leaned into the wagon to mitigate its rocking.

The ceiling was closer than Kirk expected. He sensed more than felt stone passing close above him, and ducked his head while simultaneously reaching out to orient himself. His hand rapped sharply against what felt like exposed stone. Just that quickly, he found his equilibrium and balanced himself easily with one hand on the ceiling and both feet planted on the rickety little cart.

"Know anything about architecture?" he asked George as he cranked up the charge on his phaser.

The older man snorted so forcefully that Kirk felt it jolt through the cart underneath him. "This is a hell of a time to worry about that."

"Just wondering if we were going to get the whole building falling down on our heads."

George shifted himself to steady the cart a little better, then snorted again. "Like I said, a hell of a time."

Whatever material the Grexxen had used to make the ceiling, it vaporized briskly under the phaser's beam. Kirk started his cut as far out from the cart as he could safely stretch, going by sound and stench to tell when he'd cut through all the levels of stone and timber, and up into open air. When he was only two thirds of the way around a modest circle, a fracture as wide as his hand opened up opposite his cut with a *crack!* like a shot from a Vragax rifle. Kirk recoiled away from the collapsing flap, calling, "Heads up!" a moment too late to serve any real purpose. A startling mass of wires, wood, and concrete crashed down just beyond the nose of the cart, throwing up a choking cloud of pulverized stone and plastic. Kirk covered his mouth and nose with one hand and turned away from the wreckage until the worst of it had settled.

Below him, George Kirk coughed to clear his lungs, but didn't let go of the cart handles. When he could talk again, he commented hoarsely, "Well, the building didn't fall down."

Not so far, at least. Edging up to the end of the cart, Kirk leaned out to hook his hands over the phaser-cut rim of the hole. "Stay out of the way until I tell you it's all clear." It felt ludicrous to worry about the noise now, but he still felt awkward speaking in a normal tone. "And keep your phaser ready in case we have to make a quick retreat."

George held up the weapon in curt acknowledgment, and Kirk pulled himself up through the hole.

The first thing he noticed was the brightness of the atrium, lit from the fires out on the quad. Images of flame danced murkily through layer upon layer of smoky glass panels, peeking into the building without actually rushing inside. Kirk hoped his phaser fire hadn't been as readily visible to the Vragax as their fires were to him. Then, just as he levered himself up onto his knees on the lip of the hole, he noticed the sound of breathing. Not his own breathing. He froze even before he felt the cool touch of a gauss rifle against the back of his skull.

"Don't shoot." He said it remarkably calmly, even

to his own ears. It wasn't worth sounding desperate. If it was a Vragax behind him, it wouldn't matter what he said; if it was a human, the sound of another human's voice should be enough to save him.

At least, that's what he thought.

But the gauss rifle against his neck never wavered. "Ah," said a voice that somehow managed to be oddly familiar and yet coldly unrecognizable all at the same time. "So this is the great Captain Kirk."

Sulu didn't remember the caverns on Tlaoli being this *cold* before. The fierce wind that hit them as they descended into the dusky twilight of the sinkhole entrance should have warned him, but although he heard Sanner groan and young Ensign Chekov bite off a dismayed gasp, Sulu didn't connect the strong flow of air to the temperature gradients that must exist underground. It wasn't until the nano-woven fibers of his caving suit expanded to their full insulating thickness before they'd even reached the end of the narrow tube twisting down from the sinkhole floor that Sulu realized this expedition was going to be as physically painful as it was dangerous. By the time they dropped down the final ropes to the massive rubble pile that gave them access to the ancient alien-constructed conduits, the exposed skin on Sulu's face already felt stiff and wind-burned. That tight, raw feeling reminded him of the subarctic night he'd endured back when he'd been stranded by that transporter malfunction on Alfa 117. God, had that been only a few weeks ago? Between the alien virus he'd caught at Psi 2000 and his excursion twenty-five years into his own future at Basaraba, Sulu felt as if that freezing night on Alfa 117 had happened to another person entirely.

And if they didn't get the timeline fixed, that was going to be literally true.

*"Man,* it's cold! Taking out those satellites must have really overcharged the power storage banks down here." The firefly glow of Zap Sanner's carbide lamp traced a startling cascade of skips and bounces through the darkness as he went clattering down the steep ramp of cave rubble. For a startled moment, Sulu thought the geologist had fallen, then Sanner's cheerful voice came booming back up to them. "Come on, you guys! It's not *that* slippery."

"Curb your enthusiasm, Mr. Sanner." Spock's shadowy figure descended the uneven rock surface with smooth, easy strides that got him to the bottom almost as quickly as the cave geologist's reckless scramble. "Please recollect that our mission here is to surprise the Shechenag at the Janus Gate, not to announce our arrival several minutes in advance."

"Sorry, Commander," Sanner said, then added with typical scientific temerity, "You know we're over a kilometer away from them here, don't you?"

"Indeed," answered Spock coldly. "What I do *not* know is the maximum distance at which the Shechenag's cybernetic technology can detect sounds. Do you?"

"Uh, no, sir."

Neither the geologist nor anyone else on their team spoke above a muffled whisper after that, but the frozen cave made noisy conversation for them. The ice that had once been cave runoff cracked and popped against the unyielding template of the limestone walls, and occasionally boomed in the distance as it expanded inside frozen springs and crevices.

Sulu angled the surprisingly small beam of his primitive carbide light down toward the jagged, crevassed rock pile and began to pick his way down the slope. The teenage James Kirk went past him in an agile series of jumps and leaps, although he managed to restrain the enthusiastic whoops that would have doubtless accompanied his downward rush in any other circumstance.

After a moment, a second spot of light crept over to augment Sulu's, closely followed by a third. He glanced up, half-expecting to see the older versions of himself and Chekov, but it was the younger Russian who joined him, followed by the stocky female security guard, Yuki Smith, whose stride seemed to be thrown out of balance by the heavy load of weapons and power-packs she carried. The three of them made better progress by combining the glows of their lights, but they were still the last ones to the bottom. Even Giotto managed to get there before they did despite being burdened with a phaser rifle, and the older Sulu and Chekov were already striding off toward the exit, dimly aglow with Sanner's and Spock's waiting lights.

"Sorry, guys," said Smith ruefully. Most of their pauses had been made to give her better light so she could find secure footing down the slope. "You can go ahead of me now if you want."

"No, thanks." It wasn't easy to see the younger Chekov's face under the steady flame of his carbide lamp, but his voice was dry. "I'd rather talk to you than to myself, if you understand my meaning."

"He is sort of grim and morbid," Smith agreed as they moved onward into the ice-sheathed corridors of the alien conduits. The last time Sulu had walked down this twisting ribbon of passageway, it had been filled with a floating mist of melted ice and he had been filled with relief at having just escaped Tesseract Fortress. Now he winced, remembering a rainy tropical night and a harsh Russian voice informing him that he and Chekov were the last two humans left alive on Basaraba.

"You'd be like that, too, if you'd been through what he has," Sulu said in defense of the man he'd gotten to know in that dark future. "It's only been a few days since every single member of his starship crew was killed trying to stop a Gorn invasion."

He heard Yuki Smith take in an abashed breath, but what he could see of Chekov's face didn't look as impressed. "They were *your* starship crew, too," he pointed out. It was a measure of how much Sulu had adapted to this strange doppelganger existence that he understood which version of himself the young Russian meant. "And you're not anything like him. *You* don't walk around snapping at people and scowling all the time."

This time Sulu heard the emotion below the critical surface of Chekov's voice, an uneasy mixture of embarrassment, regret, and fear. *Is that what I'm going to grow up to be?* was the question he was really asking, whether he knew it or not. *Will I turn out like that no matter what future I end up living through?*

For a moment Sulu wasn't sure what to say, but then an inner twinge of realization gave him the answer. For all of Captain Sulu's calm demeanor and bittersweet smile, there was still an unbridgeable gulf between him and his younger self. And Sulu's inexplicable shyness around the older man had come from his subconscious mind recognizing that fact, even if his intellect did not.

"Actually, I think my older self is *exactly* like yours," he told Chekov in a voice made more intense by the need to keep it down to a murmur. "Mine just knows how to hide what's happened to him a little better than yours does."

"I bet that's because he was the captain," Smith offered with surprising insight. "He's used to hiding what bothers him."

"Is that what it's like to be a starship captain?" The voice from the shadows beside them startled Sulu, and not just because of its unexpected proximity. Young Kirk emerged from behind a shattered fall of ice and rock that the rest of their party had already scrambled past. From Chekov's guilty upward glance, Sulu guessed this was the waterfall he had fallen down to inadvertently discover the alien artifacts that lay beneath the natural Tlaoli caverns. "You have to hide everything bad that happens to you so no one ever knows?"

The young man who would someday be their own starship captain—if their mission here succeeded—didn't sound upset or intimidated by that thought, Sulu noticed. But he did seem a little startled, perhaps by the realization that a captain had to be more than just a brave and brilliant hero.

"Not necessarily." Sulu had spent a fair amount of time, since discovering that at least one future version of himself had made the jump to captaincy, thinking about this question. "You have to do *whatever* needs to be done to make sure your ship carries out her mission. And that means never letting the people below you see that you've given up, even if you have."

The young man stared at him with hazel eyes whose sudden fire reflected more than just the flames of their carbide lamps. "It would be easier to do that if you never *did* give up," Kirk said, then swung away to scramble over the ice blocking the conduit as if embarrassed by his own sincerity.

They followed him down the corridor into a silent world of utter cold. The wind had died away now that they had reached the heart of the cavern's chill, and the crackling conversation of newly formed ice had been left far behind. The still air was as clear and sharp as crystal and almost as painful to breath. The glow of their carbide lamps seemed to carry a little farther in it, or so Sulu thought until Smith nudged Chekov with an elbow and whispered, "The lights are back on."

Sulu followed her gaze to the side of the cavern and saw the muted glow of alien blue illumination running along the sides of the conduit. That hadn't been there the last time he'd walked these corridors, but then the Janus Gate had been drained of its stored power by the transfer of himself and Chekov from the future. He'd expected the gate itself to be brighter on this trip, since they'd deliberately recharged it by letting it drain the Shechenag satellites in order to deactivate them, but he hadn't expected the entire cave system to come alight with the same blue glow.

"They're brighter this time," Chekov noted. "I wonder if—"

*"Zakritim, durak!"* Whatever those Russian words actually meant, their icy snap struck Sulu and Smith just as silent as the red-faced younger Chekov. "From here on, no sound!"

The rest of their party was waiting for them just around the curve of the conduit. Spock and Giotto were in the lead now, the security chief with his phaser rifle armed and ready beneath one shoulder. A slightly chastened-looking Kirk had been tucked firmly between Captain Sulu and Zap Sanner, several steps behind the leaders. The older version of Chekov motioned them to go on, but lingered toward the back, as if he needed to keep an eye on the last three members of the team. Sulu felt his own face warm and tighten a little, despite the arctic chill of the air. Ensign Chekov no longer even looked embarrassed—his face had taken on a stolid stiffness that probably meant he wished he was anywhere but here. For the first time, he looked startlingly like his older self.

The glow brightened as they continued down the ice-sheathed passage, until the walls and ceiling shone like blue mirrors in its glare. Craning his head to see around the rest of the group, Sulu caught a reflected glimpse of something black and angular on one of those bright walls. He bit down on the warning he badly wanted to shout to Spock and Giotto, and instead grabbed the older Chekov urgently by the shoulder and pointed at the image. The Russian gave him a quick, decisive nod, then vaulted past Kirk and Sanner with surprising speed and force to catch Spock and Giotto before they could round the corner ahead of them.

The young Kirk turned to look eagerly at them. "What is it?" he mouthed without making a sound. Sulu shook his head and Chekov gave him a quelling look, but Yuki Smith put out her hand and wriggled her fingers in a silent imitation of a spider crawling. Kirk nodded and squared his coltish shoulders as he glanced ahead again. When the time came for hand-to-hand combat, Sulu thought, it was going to be hard to make sure that young man kept himself safely out of the way.

Spock had advanced his tricorder around the corner and now drew it back again to check its readings. His eyebrows lifted at what he read, and he turned to give the rest of the team a familiar Starfleet hand signal: *wait until further notice.* Sulu watched him and Giotto disappear around the corner with slow and watchful steps, the security chief with his rifle at the ready. But no shriek of phaser fire or crackle of Shechenag electric weapons echoed back to them. After a long moment, a crunch of footsteps returned, and Giotto reappeared just long enough to give them another silent hand signal: *advance with caution, the way is clear.*

This time, Sulu accompanied Zap Sanner down the passageway. His older counterpart had pushed forward to catch up with young Kirk, who was nearly treading on the older Chekov's heels in his eagerness to see what lay ahead. Sulu was relieved to see that both older officers kept a strategic distance from Giotto to make sure the boy did not plunge headlong into danger. As it turned out, however, their precautions weren't needed. Around the corner, Spock was scanning his magnetically shielded tricorder slowly over a knee-high pile of jointed metal legs and sensors that had once been a Shechenag robot guard. Ice was already starting to accumulate around its crumpled form, and there was no sign of lights or activity anywhere on it.

"Its power supply has been completely drained," the Vulcan science officer reported in a low but audible voice. "Any additional robot guards that lie between us and the Janus Gate are most likely in a similar condition. Follow me."

Their advance this time was considerably less slow and cautious, although it remained scrupulously silent. As they exited the last of the narrow conduit, the alien light rose to a phosphorescent glare that made Sulu shield his eyes with one hand and wish he'd brought some kind of polarizing lenses for protection. He wondered why the team members who'd seen the Tlaoli time transporter in action before hadn't warned the rest of them to expect this. Until he caught the troubled looks on the faces of Sanner and Smith. His gaze slid past them to the younger Chekov, who gave him back a quick shake of his head, as if he had guessed what the pilot was thinking. Sulu read his answer just as easily: This was something none of them had seen before.

The Janus chamber, which Sulu remembered being full of mist and shadows, was seething now with brightness. The illumination glittered off icy walls and made a fiery blue lake of the frozen floor. And it didn't all come just from the blazing heart of the Janus Gate. All around the dark metal device, wisps and shreds of sizzling blue swept the air like billowing shreds of ash blown by an unfelt wind. The chamber looked as if it should be hot as a phaser torch, but the cold emanating from that phosphorescent light was actually so intense that it burned against Sulu's cheeks.

"Fascinating," said Spock as he stared into the glare. From the expression on Giotto's face, Sulu guessed that was not exactly the word the security chief would have chosen to describe what he was seeing. "It appears you were right, Mr. Sanner. The Shechenag satellites must have had larger energy cores than I estimated from their force field output. We have clearly overcharged the power storage systems on the time transporter."

"*And* how," was the geologist's awed response. "Is there any space left to walk around in that mess?"

"I believe so, but it is not great." Spock leaned out a little into the glare and eyed the edges of the cavern. Sulu could see a ring of evenly spaced crumpled robots there, the remnants of a Shechenag perimeter guard. "Mr. Giotto and Mr. Smith, what is the status on your power supplies?"

The security chief glanced at his rifle, then let out a muffled curse. "Down to zero already," he said. "But it was fully charged a few moments ago!"

Yuki Smith went down on one knee behind Sulu, the younger Chekov squatting beside her to help her shed and open her heavy pack. She scrambled among the power supplies she had brought, then gave Spock a troubled glance. "The ones with the magnetic shielding are all right, sir. All the rest are dead."

Spock nodded somberly. "Please attach a shielded power supply to your rifle, Mr. Smith, and station yourself in this archway with it. You will be our lookout."

"Do we *need* a lookout, Commander?" asked

Giotto. "If none of the Shechenag's mechanics can survive the power drain in here—"

"We will be safe from attack for as long as the Janus Gate remains charged," Spock agreed. "However, the Shechenag may have retreated only as far from the Janus Gate as the chamber above, which is where they were waiting when we brought Lieutenant Sulu and Commander Chekov back from the future. As soon as we exhaust the gate again by sending James Kirk and his escort to the past, we may find ourselves once again confronting them." His glance swept past the older Sulu and Chekov to rest on their younger counterparts. "At that point, with Mr. Giotto and I locked into the Janus device, it will be up to you to guard us from any interruption. You must prevent that, at any cost. If we are interrupted, there is a strong probability that we will lose all chance of retrieving Captain Kirk from the past. Do you understand?"

"Aye-aye, sir!" Chekov said, the unthinking response of a cadet responding to a drill order. Sulu saw the older Russian give him an odd, rueful look, but he made no comment in either Russian or English.

"Aye, sir," Sulu echoed. "Do you want us here, or stationed around the outside of the chamber?"

"If the Janus Gate continues to absorb power, anywhere you stand inside that chamber might become the site of a subspace rift," Spock replied. He carefully adjusted his bulky tricorder so it lay against the front of his caving suit, then looked past Giotto at the older Captain Sulu. "You remember the protected channel that leads to the viewing slot. It will doubtless be much narrower now than it was before." He widened his address to include the older Chekov and young Kirk, as well as a frowning Giotto. "When you follow Captain Sulu, stay as close to the cavern walls as possible, with your arms held tight to your sides. Any straying into the field of light around the Janus Gate could pull you into a subspace instability without warning. Walk exactly where Captain Sulu walks. Do not cut any corners or take your eyes off the person in front of you. Is that clear?"

"Aye, sir," said Giotto, echoed by the older Chekov and, a little hesitantly, by young James Kirk as well. Then the teenager glanced over his shoulder toward the younger Chekov, obviously trying for a casual, grown-up good-bye.

"Thanks," he said. "For showing me the ship, and everything."

Despite his best efforts, the stress of the moment made his adolescent voice break, shifting it momentarily into a much stronger tenor. It sounded like their own lost captain speaking to them, and for a moment even Spock looked startled. Kirk swallowed and turned back toward the older Chekov and Spock. "Ready when you are," he said bravely. And although his voice had gone back to its usual boyish register, Sulu could still hear the echo of the man he'd someday grow up to be.

The older Sulu nodded and edged his way out into the Janus chamber, brushing the wall with one shoulder and keeping himself angled to stay almost parallel with that metallic surface as he went. Giotto followed, with Kirk and the older Chekov close behind. Spock waited until they were most of the way around the perimeter of the cavern, then began circling the other way. Just as he reached the channel of clear air that Sulu could see glimmering off to the left, the Vulcan made an odd gasping sound and stopped.

"Spock, what's wrong?" the older Sulu demanded from across the chamber. "Sulu, can you see him?"

"It is... insignificant." There was a harsh tone to Spock's voice that contradicted his words, but after another moment he continued on his way to the dark alien device in the center of the cavern. Sulu stood on tiptoe, bracing himself against Chekov's shoulder as he peered through the glare, but he couldn't detect any visible wounds or injuries on the Vulcan's tall figure.

"He looks all right," he told his waiting older self. "But he's moving a little slower than before."

"I did not impact any part of the Janus field, if that is what concerns you." The harshness was fading slowly from Spock's voice, replaced by a distinct note of asperity. "Some of the Shechenag robots have mechanical cutting appendages with extremely sharp blades. I happened to encounter one of them."

"Step over that," the older Chekov said to Kirk quietly, and Sulu heard the young man's boots crunch on ice as he obeyed. The older Sulu continued picking his slow and careful way through the shifting billows of blue light, until he stood inside the curving gyroscopic arms of the alien time transporter. He drew Giotto in beside him, then carefully directed Kirk and Chekov to stand as close together as they could in back.

"You have to hold onto these arm-supports," the former starship captain told the security chief. "Don't let go, no matter what you see. It will look like you've beamed somewhere completely different, but you won't really be there. You'll still be able to hear and talk to Spock."

"Understood," the other man said, so shortly that Sulu guessed that the inferno he was facing had unnerved him. "I'm holding on."

Sulu glanced across the central fire to the lone figure on the other side. "We're ready when you are, Mr. Spock."

"One moment. I need to adjust my calculations to take into account the higher power levels we have inadvertently created." Spock's fingers flickered across the alien device's control panel with their usual velocity. "I have located what appears to be a major life-crisis, Mister Giotto. What do you see?"

"It's dark, really dark. And closed in, like a cave or a mine. I can't smell really well, but there seems to be some kind of chemical or acid in the air...This isn't Grex, Mr. Spock."

"Very well. I am adjusting the controls." There was a pause. "What do you see now, Mr. Giotto?"

"Fires in the distance. Tall buildings, all dark because there's no power, and streets full of people running...yes, *this* is Grex. But I don't remember ever standing in this particular street."

"That is because I have adjusted the controls to send you some distance away from the place where you were injured. I do not want to further complicate the timestream by having your crewmates see two of you," Spock replied. "Does your current location look like a relatively safe location?"

"It's pretty well deserted," Giotto said doubtfully, "But in this city, on *this* night...there's really no safe place to send us."

"It's all right, Mr. Giotto." That, surprisingly enough, was young Kirk. "Once we're there, I'll be able to get us to the embassy to meet my dad. I spent all summer wandering Sogo city instead of studying astrophysics like I was supposed to..."

"Then it will be up to you, James Kirk, to get yourself back to your proper place," Spock replied soberly. "I am engaging associative transport now."

Blue-white light flared lightning-sharp inside the Janus chamber, followed by a thundercrack as startled air slammed into the space formerly occupied by bodies. *Four* bodies, Sulu realized in shock and sudden despair. He didn't know whether Chief

Giotto had forgotten to hold onto the stabilizing supports, or whether the overcharged Janus Gate had simply malfunctioned. Either way spelled disaster.

Having sent both young Kirk and Chief Giotto into the past, there was now no way at all to bring their own version of Captain Kirk back to the present.

# Chapter Seven

"CHEKOV?" Kirk's brain volunteered the identification so rapidly that even he barely understood what connection he'd heard between the chillingly calm voice and the shy boy Spock had picked out for the landing party earlier that morning. When he turned to look down the barrel of the rifle, though, what he found was a man at least fifteen years older than himself with only a physical resemblance to the boy whose map Kirk had buried at the edge of the forest just a few hours ago. The person behind the dark eyes was clearly someone else entirely.

"Commander Chekov..." Antonio Giotto moved smoothly around into this strange, older Chekov's view, his own gauss rifle primed and humming. "Sir,

I'd suggest you put that gun down, or you're not going to see *any* version of the future."

The look Chekov angled at Kirk's security chief suggested he might almost enjoy seeing Giotto try to make good on that threat, but he didn't resist when the third member of their party stepped forward and pushed the muzzle of his rifle to one side.

"You'll have to forgive my first officer, Captain. We've been dodging Grexxen natives for the last couple of hours, and it's made us all a little jumpy."

Kirk thought that he ought to be more startled to find an older Sulu in the company of this older Chekov, but all the other strangeness he'd encountered since leaving Psi 2000 was beginning to make him numb to new surprises. Instead, his attention had locked on the young boy at the very back of their group. Better rested than Kirk was himself, and sealed into a dark gold cave suit not unlike the one Kirk had ditched upon first arriving on Grex. In so many ways, this was the face he still saw in the mirror. It was the face he would see even if he lived to be a hundred years old.

Apparently realizing that they were both staring, the boy tossed off what he no doubt thought was a nonchalant wave. Kirk lifted his own hand in reply.

"Captain Forester?" George Kirk's loud whisper cut across these bizarre introductions. "Captain, is everything all right up there?"

"Forester?" Sulu asked, eyebrows raised. But it was a practical question, not condescending.

Climbing to his feet, Kirk gestured toward the boy

they were all obviously protecting. "It didn't seem wise to try and explain who I am." While Sulu nodded his understanding, Kirk leaned over the hole he'd made in the floor and called down quietly, "Everything's fine, Commander. It's just a few of my men." He couldn't help stealing another look back at the boy, and found himself still under his younger self's scrutiny. "And they do have your son." As often tonight as he'd spoken with George Kirk about his son, it hadn't truly felt weird until this moment, when there was actually a physical boy to be both the object of Kirk's search and Kirk himself.

George's voice was sharp with worry and relief. "Jimmy?"

"I'm fine, Dad." The boy drew up alongside Kirk, studiously not making contact with the captain even though he leaned over the same hole to wave down at his father. "These guys took real good care of me."

Shadows drifted past on the fringe of Kirk's sight, blurred and distant through the overlapping panels of glass until they seemed almost like firelit ghosts in the darkness. Vragax on the quad outside, either wandering from place to place or patrolling the edges of the open area they'd adopted as their camp. The immediacy of danger burned away whatever strangeness Kirk still felt at meeting himself and these temporally altered versions of his crew. "Let's move this downstairs before we find ourselves with company."

The boy swung himself down through the hole too quickly for anyone to insist on helping him, followed almost immediately by Chekov and finally Sulu. Kirk listened for the neat thump and slide of each of them using the angled flower cart to catch their weight and guide them to the ground. Outside, Vragax singing swelled giddily in the distance, then receded.

"Mr. Giotto..." Kirk held out his hand to take Giotto's rifle so the chief could climb down.

The security man only shook his head and took a modest step backward, the rifle angled across his chest. "Sorry, sir. You first."

It was so much the answer Kirk would have expected that he had to smile. "Apparently, you, at least, are *my* Mr. Giotto."

"Yessir."

"I'm sure you've got one hell of a report for me."

"Oh, yessir."

By the time he and Giotto had joined the others down below, a cloud of light warmer and stronger than from George's antique tricorder screen pooled around the little group. Kirk recognized the smell of acetylene gas even before he saw the carbide lamps in Sulu's and Chekov's hands, or heard Giotto rasp the wheel on his own lamp. Wherever they'd come from, however they'd gotten here, their cave suits and lamps made it clear that they'd passed through the same caverns on Tlaoli Kirk had. The Tlaoli power drain explained their lack of Starfleet-issue equipment, although not how they'd managed to follow him here, or how they planned to get everyone back. At least the lamps would come in handy in the equally treacherous darkness of Sogo city tonight.

On the other side of the flower cart, a step away from being swallowed by the dark, George Kirk had his son by the arm as though determined to never let the boy out of his grasp again. Kirk couldn't make out the words, but he didn't really have to—even nineteen years later, the memory of that lecture made his face burn with the same angry embarrassment he could see on the boy's face now. No matter what was said in the future, this would be at the heart of every argument between them for the next nineteen years.

"Commander."

His father jerked around at Kirk's summons, his own face stiff with embarrassment even though the darkness hid any evidence of a blush. As though noticing everyone else for the first time, he let go of his son and straightened guiltily.

Kirk didn't get as much satisfaction from his father's discomfort as his fourteen-year-old self would have expected. "We don't have time for that right now. The boy knows he made a mistake." He pinned the boy with his most severe command stare. "Don't you, Mr. Kirk?"

Not yet capable of that kind of steel, the boy only nodded slowly. "Uh... Yes, sir."

"Good. Then let's get on with business." He waved everyone away from the hole in the ceiling, just to make sure no one above would suddenly catch sight of the glow from their carbides. When they were safely tucked among a clutter of tables and chairs several meters away, Kirk turned to Giotto. "I'm assuming that when Mr. Spock sent you, he also sent an extraction plan."

His chief of security nodded unhappily. "The plan was for me to maintain contact with..." He glanced at Sulu and Chekov as though for assistance, then finished for himself, "...our base of operations. Once we located you, I was to return you to Mr. Spock while Mr. Chekov and Mr. Sulu escorted your... Commander Kirk and his son to safety."

Implying that the older men wouldn't be coming back with them. At least not right away. When Kirk looked a silent query toward Sulu, the other man responded without elaborating on that aspect of Giotto's summary. "Unfortunately, we seem to have experienced an equipment malfunction. We lost contact with Mr. Spock almost immediately."

And presumably a simple communicator wouldn't be enough to solve that complication. "So I take it Mr. Spock...isn't here?" He couldn't think of a better way to phrase what he wanted to know without saying too much in front of George Kirk.

Sulu's answer was studiously literal. "Mr. Spock is where you left him."

Which meant Spock was *when* Kirk had left him, and not anywhere Kirk could get to by force of will. Sighing, he gave a curt nod. "Well, he managed to find me once before. We'll have to trust he can do it again. In the meantime, we've got to get these two to safety." He turned to George Kirk and his son. "The

*Eliza Mae* won't be arriving for another sixteen hours. Is there anywhere on the planet the Vragax aren't likely to visit before then?"

George frowned thoughtfully even as he shook his head. "I just planned on holing up in one of the more defensible rooms at the embassy," he admitted. "I was hoping *Eliza Mae* would get here early."

"She won't," Kirk and Giotto answered in a single voice.

Their certainty seemed to take George by surprise. "You guys aren't actually the embassy replacement team, are you?" The question had obviously been building in him for a while.

Kirk rubbed at his eyes, not looking forward to constructing a new webwork of lies. "No, we're not."

"Then who *are* you?"

"Special Forces," Chekov said without blinking. He barely looked up from topping off the load in his gauss rifle. "We're here on special assignment. We can't give you the details."

George Kirk nodded slowly, looking back toward Kirk as though this explanation cleared up a lot. "I noticed your uniform was a little different, and I wondered. You could have told me, sir."

"You're right. I should have trusted you." Although it felt strange to be apologizing for a lack of trust just for the sake of strengthening a further lie.

Before George could say anything more, a youthful voice from the center of their group asked modestly, "What about the wind farm?"

It took Kirk a moment to connect the boy's suggestion with Chekov's Special Forces lie, then his mind darted back to their original conversation, and he smiled. *This is why it's good to have a kid around.* He understood the blank looks on George's and Giotto's faces better than they did themselves. Fourteen months on the planet, and none of the adults had bothered to explore beyond the sectors assigned to them by Starfleet. In less than three months, Kirk and his brother Sam had hiked the woods beyond Sogo city so many times they could actually recognize and find individual trees. Only Kirk had been daring enough to climb the long ridge a few kilometers outside town, just to track down the source of a deep, powerful droning he and Sam had noticed a few days before. But he still remembered standing amid a forest of tall white windmills with his hands over his ears and his teeth singing from the bone-rattling hum.

"That's good," Kirk said, nodding approval at the boy. "Even if the Vragax decide to do something about the electrical situation in the city, they aren't going to do it before tomorrow, and the noise alone will keep anyone from using it as a campsite until then." He tried to picture the route up the hill through the trees, and realized it had been overwritten through time by that final image of the windmills against the sky. "Do you remember how to get there?" he asked his younger self.

The boy nodded. "Sure." Kneeling, he plucked a handful of small white flowers from a planting nearby. "The embassy's here." He placed one coin-sized blossom by his right knee. "If we're in under the Kaefen Rae courtyards, we're here." A neat little square of beheaded stems, a little ahead of him and toward his left. "That means the wind farm is this way—" He leaned far forward to tap the ground beyond both props. "—maybe an hour's walk through the trees."

"Northeast," George announced, studying the schematic.

"Will these underground passages take us that far?" Sulu asked.

*That would be too easy.* "I don't think they're that extensive." Kirk looked a question at the boy he knew had memorized the city's layout more recently than he had, and the boy shook his head with a rueful scowl. "But it will get us out from under the courtyard and away from the heavy concentration of Vragax," the captain went on. "Commander Kirk and I came in from the south, but if we head northeast from here, we should be able to find—or make—another way out once we get there."

They tucked George and the boy in the center of their group, with Kirk and Chekov leading, Sulu and Giotto bringing up the rear. It wasn't the most efficient arrangement, considering their only compass was the elder Kirk's tricorder, but even George didn't complain. He wanted to keep his son safe, and he was willing to sacrifice even his valued practicality to guarantee that result. Kirk wondered if he realized how much everyone else here was willing to sacrifice for the very same reason.

As they wound their way through the underground marketplace, individual shops, sculptures, and kiosks unfolded in the pale glow of their carbides like shells lifted out of the sand by a gently rising wave. Kirk watched his reflection ripple past in windows glazed against nonexistent weather, and he thought about the meticulously detailed villages he'd visited in caves back on Earth. What was the humanoid fascination with re-creating the surface world underground? He'd thought it a quaint relic from Earth's nineteenth century until he'd visited Grex as a boy, although he hadn't bothered to try and analyze it then. Now he wondered if it was a way to separate from the uncontrollable aspects of the world above, or just an attempt to make the underground world not seem so alien and frightening.

Kirk had a feeling he wasn't going to feel safe underground again for a very long time.

He stole a glance at the man pacing silently next to him, and thought about a very similar younger man who had been walking with him when this all began.

"Ensign Chekov was with me when I was...displaced." He tried not to stare too frankly at his companion. "I take it he was sent somewhere else, too?"

The question seemed to take Chekov by surprise. "I wouldn't know about that," he answered gruffly. A discomfitted frown crossed his face, and he seemed to struggle with himself for a moment before finally adding, "But he was fine when we left. He's with Mr.

Spock and the others." He looked at Kirk with an interest that was more clinical than curious. "You've been gone from them for more than two days. In my reality, you never existed at all."

"Because my younger self was...removed."

"Apparently." Chekov turned his attention forward again. "You mean a great deal to those people. They're risking everything to make sure you're reinstalled in their timeline, just like before." He made no effort to hide the bitterness in his tone. "I hope to hell you're worth it."

A sliver of light, as thin as a hair but blindingly bright, slashed down the edge of Kirk's vision like lightning. He heard George take a sharp breath behind him, but was already bolting aside and waving at the others to follow suit. "Kill the lights! Take cover!"

Whether it was the hours on Grex already spent dodging the enemy or experience from past battles Kirk could only imagine, Chekov and Sulu had responded as quickly and instinctively as Kirk. Carbides went out even as they darted for cover on either side of the cobbled path, and Kirk saw George and his son disappear inside a kiosk full of colored scarves just before the tricorder's face snapped shut and killed its own light.

The darkness didn't last. Light flooded the path they'd just abandoned, spilling from a broad door that hadn't existed even a moment before. Where the wall had split between two empty shops, four huge figures lumbered out into the market with a trio of

Vragax trailing solicitously at their heels. Kirk would have recognized the Orions even if he hadn't heard the roar of their voices or seen the flash and clash of their golden ear- and nose-rings. Orion males carried a smell about them as distinctive as their jade-colored skin and dreadlocked beards—the smell of their sulfur-rich homeworld, and too many months crowded into pirate vessels overloaded with spices and ores. Even if they had intended to pass through the marketplace with any kind of stealth, they would have been hard-pressed to reach the surface unnoticed.

By the time the Orions had rounded the bend and their voices had faded into the subterranean distance, the door from which they'd emerged had sealed itself shut as though never having been there at all. Even so, Kirk waited a full five minutes for the smell of their passage to fade before thumping Chekov on the shoulder as a signal to relight his carbide.

"I thought the Orions had been gone from Grex for more than a year." Kirk stared down the path after them, his nerves still insisting they were dangerously close for all that his nose and ears told him otherwise.

Giotto stood from behind a raised garden bed. "So did I."

"And I could have sworn we'd found all the stashes where the Orions hid their pirated contraband." George swung his tricorder back and forth over the now nonexistent door, playing impatiently with the sensitivity controls. "This one must be shielded seven ways from Sunday if even our ship's sensors didn't pick it up."

"Maybe it's not a full-fledged stash," Kirk said. "Maybe it's just the equivalent of an Orion safe house."

George shook his head and turned the tricorder around so Kirk could see its face. "That's no safe house, sir. I may not be picking up anything now that this door is sealed, but the tricorder got a real clear warp core reading for as long as it was open." He hooked a thumb back over his shoulder, his expression tense with excitement. "Captain Forester, there's a spaceship inside that hole."

This was not the first time Uhura had been left in command of the *Enterprise.* As the chief communications officer, she stood fourth in line behind Spock and Mr. Scott as a ranking line officer, and she'd often taken the conn when the senior officers were summoned to sector meetings or other planetary duties. Usually, those were times when the *Enterprise* was stationed in orbit around some stable civilian planet or Federation starbase, not on a desperate deep-space mission with a hostile alien race nearby. But Chief Engineer Montgomery Scott had spent the past two days almost continuously on his feet, first overseeing the repairs to the ship's warp engines, then taking Spock's place on the bridge while the Vulcan joined the planetary team in the search for Captain Kirk. By the time they'd managed to deactivate the Shechenag defense network and send a third expedition to Tlaoli to return young Kirk to his proper time, the tall Scotsman was literally swaying with exhaustion. Dr. McCoy, in one of the periodic visits he tended to make to the bridge during times of crisis, had declared the chief engineer no longer fit for duty and hauled him away for some much-needed sleep. Scott had agreed to go, with one adamant provision.

"If for any reason you can't stay in command of the bridge, lass," he told Uhura blearily, "for God's sake, just don't leave Riley with the conn. After what I've been through the past two days, I don't want to have to cold-start those engines ever again!"

Uhura glanced from the communications station over to the helm, hoping Kevin Riley hadn't heard that jaundiced comment. The young navigator's defensively hunched shoulders told her that he had. It was hard not to feel sorry for him. While other victims of the Psi 2000 virus such as Sulu and Spock had spent the last two days immersed in the urgent quest to recover their missing captain, Kevin Riley had remained cooped up on the *Enterprise,* with nothing to do but mope over his recent all-too-public escapade in the engine room. As soon as this crisis was over, Uhura thought, she would have to invite Riley out to dinner with some friends who could cheer him up. Robert Tomlinson and Angela Martine would be willing to help, she was sure, and perhaps she could ask Ensign Chekov and that young security guard friend of his, Yuki Smith.

Although if the time bubble they were in collapsed before they managed to get Captain Kirk back, there was no guarantee any of them would still be members of this crew. Or even still be alive.

Uhura watched the turbolift doors slide shut behind the departing chief engineer and chief medical officer, then toggled a familiar switch on her communications station. "Lieutenant Hadley to the bridge."

"Aye, sir," said the relief communications officer with surprising promptness. His next words explained why. "I'm on the ready deck now. I'll be there in just a minute."

Uhura set down her portable frequency monitor, wondering wryly if her junior officers had suspected she would soon be needing a replacement. No doubt they considered her a candidate for getting yanked off the bridge, too, after the exhausting day and night she'd spent on Tlaoli. McCoy had indeed scrutinized her very narrowly when he'd first stepped onto the bridge, but he must have had enough faith in the restorative powers of his awful-tasting nutritional supplement to leave her in command.

The turbolift hissed again, and a sandy-haired young man stepped out, still hurriedly adjusting the collar of his uniform. "Lieutenant Hadley reporting to the bridge, sir," he said before he even noticed the empty captain's chair.

"Acknowledged, Lieutenant." Uhura smiled at his startled expression. "You'll handle communications for the remainder of this shift. I'm on the conn until further notice."

"Aye, sir." Hadley waited politely for her to vacate her seat, but Uhura noticed he was already scanning the frequency monitors to see what channels she had open. "Anything special to watch for?"

"Channel three is preset for the emergency communicator Mr. Spock took with him to the planet," Uhura told him. "It's for monitoring purposes only. We're under strict orders not to hail the landing party, so the Shechenag won't suspect we've sent anyone to the planet. Conduct routine scans of all other hailing frequencies and monitor anything that seems like it might be Shechenag transmissions. I've downloaded as much of their language as the main computer could decipher into translator program nine."

"Aye, sir."

Uhura gave her boards one last assessing glance as she stood, but everything was still as it had been when Spock and Sulu had departed for Tlaoli: all subspace frequencies silent except for the natural interference that howled and chattered across the spectrum. If the Shechenag ship had left any of its crew down on the planet to guard the Janus Gate, they apparently saw no need to check in with them. Between the alien silence and Mr. Spock's ban on landing party reports, Uhura had not really had much work to do.

And now she was going to have even less.

Uhura lowered herself into the captain's chair and flexed her fingers on its broad armrests, feeling the living warmth beneath the surface. The entire command console was packed with computer circuits, giving the officer who sat there command and control of the entire starship. Despite all that power humming beneath her fingers, however, Uhura had nothing to do but gaze up at the silent copper planet on the viewscreen and wonder how long it was going to take the Shechenag to work their way back around to this side of the world. When that occurred—if it occurred—her service as substitute captain would really begin. In the meantime, she didn't even have to work at keeping the captain's seat warm.

Uhura had always known that the captain's job was the hardest on the bridge. What she hadn't realized before was that it could also be the most physically excruciating. With no screens to watch or instruments to monitor, the ship's commander had no occupation for those times when tensions were high but absolutely nothing needed to be done. Within just a few moments, Uhura caught herself tapping her fingers restively against the chair's armrests. She bit her lip, forcing her hands to relax and be still. Bored or not, she had to project the image of an alert and attentive commander, or risk losing the confidence of her crew.

Uhura had always thought Captain Kirk's tendency to stride around the bridge and consult his officers at their stations just reflected his own innate energy. Now she was starting to wonder if it was a deliberate strategy for staying watchful and alert.

"Any change in the ship's position, Mr. Riley?" she asked the lieutenant in an attempt to fill the silence.

"Nothing unusual, sir." The navigator's rigid shoulders relaxed a little as he focused on answering her question. "We're exactly on station over the planet's equatorial plane."

"No major gravitational fluctuations?"

"Just the standard bumps and potholes." Relief pilot Lieutenant Alden had clearly filled in for Sulu before, probably while the chief helmsman had been lost on Basaraba. His coffee-colored hands moved confidently over the helm controls, correcting for Tlaoli's unstable gravity fields. "In fact, the perturbations actually seem to be dying out a little."

Uhura studied the glittering force-field lines netting their way around Tlaoli, now almost complete except for the darkened patch Spock and Sulu had deactivated. Was it her imagination, or had a pearly luster begun to shine above the ancient planet's rust-red atmosphere as the Shechenag continued placing satellites on the opposite side of the world? "Maybe part of what the defensive barrier does is keep the planet from dragging any more spaceships down to its surface," she speculated. "That would prevent them from being destroyed by the force field when they were helpless to escape."

Riley gave her a curious look over his shoulder. "I thought the Shechenag were just trying to protect the timestream, sir. Why should they care if ships are destroyed by their force field, as long as nobody makes it to the Janus Gate?"

"I don't know," Uhura admitted. "But we can't assume we really understand them, Lieutenant, when we've barely been able to decode their language. Statements and actions that we've interpreted as hostile may not have been intended that way."

"I think we're about to find out if that's true, sir." A red light flashed at Alden's station. "I've got a proximity alert from the gravitational sensors. Something big is heading straight for us."

Uhura glanced across at Lieutenant Karen Tracey, filling in for Spock at the science panel. "Long-range scanner report."

"I'm not showing anything—wait, yes, I am." The technician adjusted a control at her station, altering the image on the viewscreen to an enlarged quadrant of Tlaoli's rusty disk. A familiar smudge of unlit black could just be seen crossing the dapple of distant stars. "Sorry, Lieutenant. The radiation from the force field lines completely swamped their ion output."

Uhura swung around toward Hadley at communications. "Open a channel to the Shechenag ship, using the same frequency as their previous communications." She saw the young man's hands slide across the controls as he obeyed her. "Engage the partial translator and run my voice through it before transmitting. Tell me when you're ready."

"I'm ready now, sir."

Uhura took a deep breath and turned back to the main viewscreen, in case the Shechenag opened a reply channel. "Four more hours are permitted for our departure from this system," she said, hoping the translator conveyed her attempt to be conciliatory. "We wait to see if our lost crewman returns. No hostility is intended."

There was a pause, then the viewscreen rippled to show the barren interior of the alien spacecraft's bridge. The huddle of cybernetic bodies at the center of that simple space seemed a little smaller, as if some of the controlling aliens had been dispatched on other errands. Of those remaining, two had reared their mechanical suits up on jointed legs to reveal the actual alien bodies inside, agitated as goldfish in a dropped bowl.

"This is all untruthful," said one flat voice, immediately overlapped by a second.

"This is not the native language. You have known our speech always."

*"No."* Uhura tried to make her own voice just as flat and definitive as theirs. "Our translation device is new and incomplete. We made it to communicate better, to avoid hostility."

"Hostility commenced when you damaged the blocking sphere." The first Shechenag waved several appendages, both real and robotic, to emphasize its point. The gestures seemed almost theatrically fierce in comparison with its toneless machine-generated voice. "We are Shechenag. We do not make war. This planet creates danger for all who come here. We create protection."

"Yes, we know." Uhura swept her own hands out in

a placating gesture of her own, although she wasn't sure the aliens would see or understand. She chose every word she spoke with care. "We do not wish your blocking sphere to be destroyed. The satellites which failed were destroyed by the alien machine down on the planet. We watched it drain their power."

That sparked a flurry of twitches and color changes inside several robotic torsos as their translucent occupants erupted into hisses and clatters. None of the comments were turned into English by the Shechenag's translator. Uhura glanced over her shoulder at Hadley, but the junior communications officer shook his head. Their own rough translating device couldn't sort out all the overlapping conversations well enough to decipher them.

The clattering uproar finally died away to a last few cryptic utterances: "Unsure, insecure, observe." "Remove destabilizing force." and "Protect. Protect only." The last comment seemed to be the most popular among the joint commanders of the alien ship; several of them lifted and dropped their jointed mechanical arms in a rumble of approval. Their small glimmering bodies turned pale, then clear again, as if they had voiced their emotional reaction to Uhura's words and were now calm.

"Repairs will be made to complete the blocking sphere," the first Shechenag said while others detached various insectoid robots from their bodies and sent them scuttling out of sight, perhaps to communicate their new plan of action to the rest of their crew.

"No approach or maneuver will be permitted at this time. Immediate departure from the system is advised."

Uhura took a deep breath, knowing that this was the really risky part. "We prefer to wait for our missing crewman. If he can return through the alien time transporter, he may be able to use a vessel already on the planet to rejoin us."

There was an alarmingly long pause, but no flutter of colorful emotion that she could see inside the translucent tank. There was a stillness to the Shechenag spokesman's cybernetic casing that Uhura thought might indicate either confusion or puzzlement. "No return is possible without intervention in the timestream," the alien said at last. "No intervention is possible without activation of the prohibited device."

"Yeah," Riley said softly, beneath his breath so the translator pickup wouldn't catch the words. "Don't think about that too hard, okay?"

Uhura hushed him with a restraining hand on his shoulder, and only then noticed that she had stood up from the captain's console without thinking and come forward to the helm to confront their opponents, just as Captain Kirk often did. She tried to think the way he would have, too, rapidly assessing and discarding the various excuses they could use to remain in the Tlaoli system without arousing the Shechenag's suspicions. She remembered the comment one of them had made during their own discussion: unsure, insecure, observe. It gave Uhura the rationale she was looking for.

"This is understood," she said. "We will make no maneuvers or approaches to the planet. But if it is permitted, we wish to observe the completion of the blocking sphere to assure our leaders that no further disruptions will occur in the timestream."

There was a brief exchange of clicks among the group crouched around the speaker, then its translucent tank lifted so that the naked swimmer inside could look more directly at Uhura through whatever version of a viewscreen the cybernetic aliens used. "This is logical and permitted," the Shechenag said. "Completion of the shield is estimated in point zero six five planetary rotations."

And with that, the viewscreen blanked out for a moment, then returned to its normal display of space dusted with stars and Tlaoli's sunlit face shining like a polished copper coin in the distance. Uhura frowned up at the ancient planet, but her tired brain just wouldn't do the math computation she needed. She finally turned to Lieutenant Karen Tracey.

"How long is point zero six five rotations in our units?"

The science technician made Uhura jealous by not even glancing at her monitor before she answered. "Given the length of Tlaoli's day, approximately an hour and a half, sir."

Uhura bit her lip again, this time to suppress an exclamation that it wouldn't be dignified to make in front of her crew. She watched the dark smudge of the alien starship cross the stars, then leap into high relief as it passed over Tlaoli's shining surface and headed for the barren spot where ten satellites had been deactivated less than an hour ago. So far, they'd been successful at keeping the presence of their landing party concealed, but that wasn't going to do them the slightest bit of good if the shuttle found itself trapped under a completed force shield.

None of Uhura's options now were appealing. If she allowed the Shechenag to go about their work, the shuttle *might* make it out in the meantime without any intervention on her part. But if they didn't, the *Enterprise* would be forced to blast apart the protective blockade to free their shuttle crew. There was no way to know if they could destroy this unknown alien technology, and even if they did, such an overt act of hostility might gain the Federation a new and dangerous enemy in this sector of space. On the other hand, if Uhura intervened before the blockade was completed, they would probably still make enemies of the Shechenag and possibly endanger their landing party even more. As fearful as the ancient aliens were of time disruptions, she wouldn't be surprised if they tried to seize the shuttle as it left Tlaoli, or even tried to attack the Janus Gate itself.

For one craven moment, Uhura considered asking Hadley to summon Commander Scott to the conn, but she knew the exhausted chief engineer wouldn't be any better than she was at sorting through their limited options. With a sigh, she sank back into the captain's chair and tried to make herself think like Kirk.

"Lieutenant Alden, I don't suppose you observed any of the maneuvers Commander Spock and Lieutenant Sulu used to deactivate those defensive satellites."

The relief pilot threw an almost incredulous look over his shoulder. "Sir, I wouldn't have missed that show for all the dilithium on Vulcan! When the word went out about what they were planning to do, the entire helm section headed for the auxiliary bridge and rigged the viewscreen down there to watch the lieutenant fly that mission."

Uhura gave him a somber look. "Do you think we could carry out that maneuver again if the Shechenag close up the gap in the satellite network?"

Alden didn't even hesitate. "Never," he said. "I didn't even believe the lieutenant could fly that well off instruments until I saw him do it. And no one else on board can handle this ship the way he can. No one."

Kevin Riley swung around from the navigation station to join the discussion. "There also isn't anyone else on board besides Commander Spock who could figure out the transporter angles to that kind of precision. Those satellites are only about the size of an escape pod, and right now we're about ten thousand kilometers away from them. Aiming just to hit them would be hard enough—trying to bounce the beam off them and then down to a precise spot on the planet's surface is statistically impossible."

Uhura frowned up at the viewscreen. A tiny puff of reflected sunlight beside the Shechenag ship marked the launch of a replacement satellite, and a moment later she saw an iridescent strand of light shoot out across the stretch of empty copper sky that marked their landing party's escape route. Impossible or not, she had to make sure the hole in that barrier stayed open at all costs.

Because if it closed, they'd not only lose Captain Kirk and the six crewmen who'd risked their lives to save him, they'd also lose their entire future.

# Chapter Eight

SULU STARED for a long time at the empty space on the far side of the Janus Gate, as if just by staring hard enough he could somehow make Chief Giotto *be* there, crumpled to his knees perhaps, or obscured by the fading blue glow of the alien device. But no matter how long he looked, the space that had just a few minutes ago been occupied by young Kirk, older Chekov and older Sulu—and by the man who was supposed to maintain their link between the past and the present—stood completely and impossibly vacant.

"What the hell happened?" The voice that broke the stunned silence was Sanner's, and it sounded just as shaken as Sulu felt. "Where's Giotto?"

The tall and silent figure on the other side of the Janus Gate finally stirred, glancing down at the alien control board in front of him. "It appears the Janus Gate has displaced him to the past along with the others. The power overload must have thrown it into full transport mode without my instructing it to do so."

Yuki Smith leaned in between Sulu and Chekov, bumping both of them in the back with her phaser rifle. "Does that mean there's another Mr. Giotto back in the cave where we were stuck for so long?" she asked worriedly.

"Possibly. The gate was programmed only for viewing mode...but the power surge may have triggered an actual replacement." The noticeable hesitation in Spock's voice made Sulu wonder if the Vulcan was less sure of his deductions than usual. "Mr. Sanner, you can move more quickly through the caves than anyone else. Check the healing chamber for a light inside one of the columns." There was another, even longer pause, then an audible intake of breath before Spock resumed. "Mr. Giotto remembered being badly wounded at the time of the native uprising on Grex."

"On my way." The geologist headed off into the darkness with long, loping strides. It took a long time for the clattering sound of his footsteps to fade into the sound of dripping water and uneasy silence. Sulu watched Spock for a long time, then glanced back across the chamber at Chekov and Smith, seeing the same question in their eyes that he was feeling. Why wasn't Spock doing anything, or issuing further orders? It looked for all the world as if the Vulcan had frozen into ice at his station, although, in fact, the

Janus chamber was getting warmer and warmer all the time. Had something happened to him, perhaps some side effect of subspace radiation or the last treacherous snap of a rent tearing through space and time?

"Mr. Spock?" Sulu took a cautious step out into the chamber. The curtains of blue light that had billowed around the Janus Gate had at first seemed to be completely gone, but now they looked like they might be coalescing again in the darkness. A damp breath blew on Sulu's frost-burned face, and he stiffened in alarm until he realized what he was feeling was a cascade of mist from melting ice. The nano-woven fibers of his caving suit squirmed against his skin as they condensed down to a thinner and more water-repellent foam. Beads of moisture were already glittering on the suit's outer surface, and runnels dripped off his helmet from a layer of frost he hadn't even known was there.

"Commander Spock, are you all right?" It hadn't seemed odd at first that the Vulcan had stayed at his post beside the Janus Gate, since there was always the chance Giotto would reappear and Spock would need to adjust the controls to bring their version of Kirk back with him. But now that the device had clearly lost most of its stored power, the science officer's continuing stillness was beginning to alarm Sulu.

There was no answer. Sulu took another step out into the mist, then another. Nothing happened, so he edged around the side of the chamber in the same direction Spock had taken.

"Lieutenant Sulu!" The note of concern in that Russian voice stopped Sulu in his tracks. He glanced back over his shoulder at Chekov and Smith, barely visible now except for the misty gleams of their carbide lights. "Watch out for the Shechenag robots, sir. Mr. Spock stepped on one with a cutting blade, remember."

"Thanks, Ensign." Sulu angled his carbide light down toward his feet and saw a crumpled heap of mechanical limbs a half meter in front of him. He stepped over it carefully and continued on his way, as far as he remembered the Vulcan going before he turned to approach the alien time machine along its corridor of safety. Although the Janus Gate was now lit only by the dimmest of flickers at its heart, Sulu paused to scan the ground again and see if he could find any footprints or tracks in the icy crust.

What he saw through the flowing mist made his eyes narrow in dismay. A line of dark smudges ran across the ice, tracing a path from where he stood to the tall, silent figure beside the Janus Gate. When Sulu bent down to touch one of those marks, the frozen slush he brought up on his gloved finger glittered a distinctive green in the glow of his carbide. It was the color of Vulcan blood.

"Mr. Spock?"

Still no reply. Sulu followed the line of bloody footprints toward the first officer, feeling apprehension thud like stones inside his gut. If they lost Spock as well as Giotto, any hope of retrieving Captain Kirk was truly lost...but the closer Sulu came, the more apparent it was that Spock had not been pulled into the Gate's time-warp nor made catatonic by some unknown side effect of its use. The Vulcan's eyes were closed and his angular face was deeply intent, as if he were meditating on something profound. Sulu paused an arm's length away, remembering stories he had heard about the nearly mystical ability of Vulcans to survive even severe injuries. Maybe Spock's meditation had something to do with that.

"Is the commander all right?" That was Smith's anxious voice, echoing oddly through the curdled mist.

"I think so," Sulu said. "He looks like he's in some kind of trance right now." Sulu settled himself to wait where he was, not wanting to approach the Janus Gate any closer, yet not feeling right about leaving the Vulcan alone in this defenseless condition. "I'm not going to bother him. It's not like we can do anything but wait and see if another Giotto came out through the Janus Gate."

"What will it mean, if he did?" Chekov asked. "Can we send him back to Grex once he's healed, and then get the captain back along with our version of Mr. Giotto?"

"Maybe...but if the younger version of Giotto goes back healed instead of wounded, we'll have changed our timeline again. We'll just have to hope that's not as big a change as taking Captain Kirk out of it completely." Sulu was starting to see why the Shechenag had insisted it was impossible to repair damage to any timeline. Thinking about the cybernetic aliens reminded him abruptly that with all of the Janus Gate's stolen power discharged, the way was once again open for them to invade the caverns. "Don't forget to keep an eye on the ceiling in case the Shechenag decide to drop in on us," he reminded the junior officers.

"We can't see the ceiling through the fog, sir," Chekov pointed out. Despite the tension, Sulu found himself smiling, just a little, at the young ensign's unfailing earnestness.

"Well, just keep an eye on whatever you can see up there. And let's not talk anymore. If we're quiet, we should be able to hear those robots of theirs clattering against the rocks long before we see them."

The two young *Enterprise* crewmen fell obediently silent, not even whispering to each other in the doorway. Sulu wished he could enforce the same order on the cavern itself. As the temperature climbed, the Janus chamber began to make an entire symphony of sounds: meltwater dripping from a thousand places, then rushing and gurgling its way farther underground, the slow groan and thunderous cracking of ice detaching from the walls. As the minutes passed, the noises echoed back from the rest of the frozen caverns as well, making Sulu wonder how Spock could keep himself tranced amid the din. The only warning he had that Zap Sanner was coming back were the yelps of surprise and dismay that

Smith and Chekov made when the geologist came plunging out of the dark conduit behind them.

"Nothing." The word was spit out between tearing gasps as the geologist caught at the edge of the cavern wall to support himself. He must have run at full speed to the breakdown cavern where the alien healing chambers were, Sulu realized, through passages filled with melting ice and mist. For a long time, Sanner didn't manage to make any other sounds but gasps, but then he didn't really need to. The bleakness in that single word had told them everything they needed to know.

"You mean Mr. Giotto wasn't there?" Smith asked anyway.

Sulu could tell Sanner nodded because his carbide glow fell and lifted twice. But it took another few minutes for the geologist to regain enough breath for continuous speech. "There were no lights in any columns . . . no versions of Giotto hiding anywhere in the cavern. I even checked the ropes up to the exit, but they were all still coated with frost. No one went out that way."

"Then Giotto *wasn't* exchanged with his younger self," Sulu reflected. "I guess that's good, in a way. It means we won't have changed the timeline any further, as long as we can still get Captain Kirk and Mr. Giotto back again from the past."

"But how *are* we going to get them, sir?" Chekov demanded. "We don't have anyone left who has a connection to Captain Kirk's past—"

"Yes." Spock's voice echoed deep and strong as a church bell in the misty darkness. "We do."

Sulu took a step toward the Vulcan, seeing both alertness and pain in his expression. "Are you all right, Commander? Is there any medical treatment we can give you?"

"None that will accomplish more than I have already done," the science officer said calmly. "And it is far more important right now to address Ensign Chekov's question. I believe there is another way for us to contact Captain Kirk and Chief Giotto, but there is one major impediment to our doing so."

Sulu glanced up toward the cavern's ceiling, but saw no robotic intruders swarming down through the billowing fog. "What impediment is that?"

"Power." Spock gestured at the Janus Gate. Inside its gyroscopic arms, the light that had once been too brilliant to look directly at now flickered like a will-o'-the-wisp. "The device has used all the energy we channeled into it from the Shechenag satellites. Unless we find a way to recharge it, we will not be able to retrieve anyone from anywhere."

Between George Kirk and Antonio Giotto, Kirk had nearly fifty years of combined security experience at his disposal. As he watched them tease open the shielded Orion bulkhead using nothing but a phaser's tuning apparatus and George's antique tricorder, Kirk realized that he'd never fully appreciated all the practical skills that came with a good security specialist. Not in his own father, and certainly not in the interchangeable personnel he routinely ordered up as protection forces for his landing parties. These were handy men to have around. He hoped he'd have the opportunity to make better use of them in the future—any future.

A single stony *clunk!* announced the separation of the door's mammoth locking mechanism a mere fifteen minutes after George and Giotto had set to work on it. They backed away from the rapidly brightening entrance along with everyone else, Giotto quickly reassembling his phaser while George worked on realigning his tricorder to scan the freshly opened stash ahead of them.

"Orion locks are so useless," the older man remarked with a mixture of frustration and disgust. "If they didn't use more shielding than God on anything they thought was important, they'd be robbed by their own slave races every ten minutes."

Apparently, that shielding was enough most of the time, though. Kirk doubted that most of the races who had access to an Orion stash possessed the sort of high-end lock-picking equipment George and Giotto had just used. The ruthless practicality that made Orions such formidable enemies in combat probably also kept them from wasting any more resources than necessary, whether it was on locks or lighting or personal hygiene. He was just glad someone in this Orion cabal had seen fit to keep a ship available as an escape route.

Mazelike corridors split in all directions just past the threshold of the hidden door, smooth and modern and drilled out of the surrounding rock with all the sturdy, joisted lack of aesthetics of a crude dilithium mine. Kirk wouldn't have mistaken it for some service access to the underground Grexxen market even if he hadn't seen the effort necessary just to get inside. There was the same faintly sulfurous odor as he'd smelled on the Orions themselves, and the glaringly bright overhead lights pulsed with the disturbing reddish cast of Orion's native sun. Stepping around one of the many piles of crates and grav-sleds littering the corridor, Kirk glanced back at George and his tricorder. "Anything?"

The older man studied the readout for a moment, then shook his head. "I think I've got a pretty clear map of the facility—the shielding's all outside the main perimeter. I'm not getting any life-sign readings except for ours."

"What about the warp core?" Kirk asked.

Another minute adjustment of the device's sensors. "Still there." He used the tricorder to point down one of several possible paths. "A little more than a kilometer, that way."

Giotto stayed close to George, keeping watch for unexpected booby traps or personnel while George led them deeper into the installation using nothing but the tricorder's sensors. They stayed grouped together more closely now, since they no longer had the concealing space of the open marketplace, but they were still careful to keep the boy near the center with the adult men stationed as armed guards all around.

Kirk suspected the Orion tunnels weren't as convoluted as they seemed, but it was hard to tell around the clutter all but blocking their progress. A few steps forward turned almost immediately into an extended wriggle between stacks of equipment and supplies, and it wasn't always clear where they turned a corner or where they left the main conduit for one of its less crowded side branches. Shouldering aside a metal crate that looked almost like an upright coffin, Sulu mused aloud, "I wonder if the Orions are coming or going?"

Giotto leaned back to help him steady the box before it swayed over on top of them all. "They left more than a year ago—I was with the team that tossed the last of them out."

Kirk saw George flick a curious frown over his shoulder at Giotto, and wondered himself which of his father's young subordinates had grown up to be Kirk's chief of security. After nineteen years, Kirk only remembered three or four of George's team from Grex, and those faces were so clouded over by grief and guilt that he seldom thought about them before today. It disturbed him a little to realize how effortlessly the past could shield itself from the present.

Turning back to his tricorder, George seemed to set aside the question of Giotto's identity as yet another Special Forces enigma that he had no right to pursue. "He's right—the last of the Orions supposedly shipped out fourteen months ago. And we've had the whole planet locked down tight as a drum since then, to make sure nobody else tried to raid the contraband stashes the Orions left behind." He shook his head definitively. "There's no way the Orions or anybody else got a ship past us and landed under Sogo city without us knowing about it."

"Then these Orions have been here all along," Chekov said.

Giotto made a face that said he found the possibility unlikely. "But why? What's in it for them to hide out underground on a planet they don't even control anymore?"

The lack of interest in Chekov's shrug couldn't have been more profound. "I'm just telling you the tactical realities, based on what you're saying." He stepped aside to glance down one of the side corridors, obviously more concerned with keeping watch than actually entering into this discussion. "I have no idea what the hell's going on around here."

"No, he's right," George said thoughtfully as he picked his way around several piles of some unidentifiable ore. "If you think about it, it explains a lot. Ever since we got here, there's always been a core of Vragax who refused to cooperate in the rebuilding process, no matter how hard Starfleet tried. They'd be part of negotiations with the Kozhu about how to structure a democratic government right up to the point when they just refused to come back to the table. No explanation given. Or they'd seem to agree to a division of arable land in the southern hemisphere, then instigate nighttime raids on Kozhu settlements there." He motioned for Giotto to help him open a wider path down the middle of the hall. "After fourteen months, we'd made next to no progress in getting this planet back on its feet as a free society, all thanks to them."

Kirk remembered his father's angry tirades about the lack of native cooperation from the first time he'd been on Grex. As a boy, he'd always believed his father reacted with so much anger because he didn't think the Federation should be on Grex to begin with, and so saw every setback in the restructuring process as proof that the Federation's efforts were being wasted. It had never occurred to Kirk that the irritation George had expressed so freely in those days had been because he so badly wanted the mission to succeed and didn't know how to make that happen.

It was his younger self, though, who said with almost adult clarity, "I guess they weren't representing any real Vragax faction. The Orions were putting them up to it all along."

"We should have known the Orions wouldn't give up the planet so easily." It was the first time Kirk could remember hearing his father respond to anything his younger self said as though they were equals. "Hell, we should have known they'd try and sneak in the back door after we'd locked the front! When the violence broke out tonight, we all assumed the Vragax rebels had found a stash of Orion weapons we'd somehow overlooked. I mean, how else could they get the gauss rifles and the sonic grenades and the microbolt that took down Maione's shuttle? It never occurred to us that there had been Orions here the whole time, stirring up dissent and supplying a handful of troublemakers with weapons to guarantee the rebuilding process never got off the ground."

"I guess a few bad apples can ruin an entire planetary society." Chekov heaved one of the abandoned grav-sleds upright, then caught it with one hand before it could drift any farther down the hall. "This is all very fascinating," he said with a complete lack of sincerity, "but we still need to get you and your son off this planet." He rolled one of the metal crates onto the waiting sled. "Can we save the history lesson until later?"

Kirk nodded Giotto to stay close to George and the boy as they continued down the hall, then stepped forward to hold the sled steady while Chekov heaved another metal-sided crate on top of the first. "What are you doing?"

"Assuming the Orions are going to come back at some point." This time he waved for Kirk to help him lift a particularly heavy piece of strange equipment. "Once we find this ship, we still have to get into it and figure out if we can fly it. I thought slowing the Orions down might be a good idea."

By the time he saw the big bay door at the end of their hike, Kirk thought it might be a good idea, too. This was no flimsy Orion bulkhead, meant only to keep out a few primitive natives with stone knives and wooden spears. This was the same sort of state-of-the-art installation found on the *Enterprise*'s shuttlebay, with all the attendant check systems and safeguards.

"Get to work," he told his father and Giotto. Then he tossed a grin at Chekov and the Russian's sledful of crates and loose metal equipment and supplies. "I can see they must have had Boy Scouts back in Moscow."

He was surprised when he got a wry half smile in return. "Be prepared."

They stacked up a wall waist-high and twice that deep, lining the exterior with the more irregularly shaped pieces of heavy equipment and leaving the relatively smooth, even sides of the metal crates on the inner surface closer to the big bay door. Kirk wasn't sure how much protection the barricade would actually afford them if the Orions returned with anything more powerful than gauss rifles, but it kept them busy and out of the security officers' way.

Sulu helped Chekov wrestle the now-empty grav-sled through the gap they'd left in the barricade for that purpose. "Once we find this ship," he asked Kirk quietly, "are we sure we can actually get it out of here?"

If he'd meant the soft pitch of his voice to keep George or his son from overhearing, he was apparently unsuccessful. "Oh, it'll get out, all right," George said without looking away from his work on the door. "Every one of these stashes has at least one small escape vessel for the head Orion poobah, with a launch tube leading out to the surface."

"How small?" That was one element of their plan Kirk hadn't considered when George first reported a warp core available for hijacking at the end of this tunnel. "Will it be big enough for all of us?"

George still didn't turn around, and Kirk couldn't tell from the pause before his father answered whether George also hadn't thought about that particular detail, or whether he'd simply hoped it would end up not being an issue. "I don't know," the older man finally admitted. "The size of the ships varied in the other stashes. But don't worry—" He looked back at Kirk and the others with grim resolution. "We're not going to leave anyone behind."

Which was a laudable sentiment, Kirk thought, but didn't necessarily mean everyone would be leaving the same way.

Turning to help drag crates across the last narrow opening, Kirk asked Sulu quietly, "What exactly *is* the plan for getting the rest of us out of here?"

The other captain gave him a rueful look. "Just what your security chief said—he was supposed to stay linked with the alien transporter device so that Mr. Spock could use him as a focal point to bring you back through." He nodded across at Chekov, who continued arranging the last level of barricade in grim silence, as though he wasn't even part of their conversation. "Pavel and I were going to stay behind and make sure the boy got out of here to grow up safely."

"But Mr. Giotto lost his link to this transporter, which means Spock lost his link to us. What was Plan B?"

Sulu picked up his gauss rifle and turned it over to check its charge. "We were working with limited resources. There was no Plan B."

"Gentlemen," Kirk said gently, "Mr. Spock *always* has a Plan B."

Chekov turned from dropping the last crate into place, and Kirk thought for an instant that he glimpsed what almost looked like regret or despair in the older man's lean face. Then the tearing whistle of a gauss rifle's projectile crashed through the top edge of the barricade from outside, spraying blood and splintered metal across them all.

She couldn't watch the viewscreen anymore.

Uhura swung the captain's chair away from the ugly metamorphosis that was taking place on Tlaoli. An hour ago, the ancient planet had glowed in darkening shades of copper, garnet, and rust as the curving arc of sunset crept across its dusty sky. Now, what was left of its dayside looked like a cataract-blinded eye floating in space. The Shechenag must have completed the rest of their protective satellite barrier before discovering the hole Spock and Sulu had punched through to the Janus Gate. Now that they were repairing that hole, one satellite at a time, their force field had brightened and coalesced from spider-silk strands to a thick, opalescent shroud. The blanched planet reminded Uhura a little too much of the eerie swirling aura of Psi 2000 just before that doomed planet had exploded. She knew Tlaoli wasn't going to do anything so drastic, but if the landing team couldn't escape before the planetary defense shield was completed, the results would be far more catastrophic than the mere destruction of a planet.

Freeing her gaze from the progress of the Shechenag starship on the viewscreen also served to free Uhura's mind from the decision-making quandary that had kept her torn between action and inaction for the past hour. With only thirty minutes to go before the Shechenag completed their defensive shield, she could no longer simply wait for the shuttle to appear. She would have to assume that it wasn't going to get out in time, and react accordingly.

"Lieutenant Hadley." Uhura could tell from the way the junior communications officer spun around to meet her gaze that he was ready and waiting for the orders he expected her to give. Her next words made his reaching hand freeze in midair, however. "Call Lieutenant Kyle to the bridge at once." Before he had time to do more than look disconcerted, Uhura added with a smile, "And put the ship on yellow alert."

"Aye, sir." Hadley resumed the gesture he'd interrupted, and an instant later yellow alarm lights began to strobe across the bridge. With his other hand, he opened the intraship channel that would connect him to the *Enterprise*'s most skilled transporter technician. "Lieutenant Kyle, report to the bridge immediately. Repeat, report to the bridge immediately."

There was a way all good communications officers had of packing a wealth of meaning into the standard ship hails without ever sounding dramatic or unprofessional. Uhura had used those subtle changes in voice, pitch, and tonality so many times herself that they had become almost subconscious. Hearing them now in Lieutenant Hadley's unfamiliar male register made her suddenly aware of why Starfleet still insisted on having a human communications officer instead of assigning that work to the ship's main computer.

Hadley swung back around toward Uhura, his gaze slipping past her and up to the viewscreen, as if Tlaoli's swirling pallor was just too strange to look away from. Uhura had to clench her hands around the armrests of the captain's console to keep from glancing back herself. "Lieutenant Kyle's on his way," the junior officer said. "Lieutenant, should I hail the landing party now?"

"No," Uhura said flatly. "If Commander Spock hasn't left the planet yet, it's because Captain Kirk isn't back yet. And a communication from us saying that the satellite shield is closing won't make the Janus Gate work any better or any faster. All it will do is warn the Shechenag that someone is using it." Uhura turned toward Karen Tracey at the science station. "What we have to do is make sure that shield *doesn't* close until the shuttle is on its way back to us. And for that, we'll need the best fix on the Janus Gate that your long-range scanners can give us, Lieutenant."

"Aye, sir." The technical officer ducked back over her display screens.

Uhura swiveled back toward the helm, keeping her gaze on the two men there rather than on the ominous pale crescent that hung on the viewscreen above them. "Riley, I need you to keep track of that Shechenag starship on a meter scale if possible. Can you do that?"

"Aye, sir." All of the self-consciousness had left the young navigator's voice as he manipulated his instruments to triangulate on a moving target rather than a distant lodestone star. "Got it, sir."

"Send the coordinates over to helm and engineering. Tracey, your coordinates for the Janus Gate need to go to the same two bridge stations." Uhura suspected Captain Kirk wouldn't have given the crew his directions all helter-skelter like this, but her mind was racing so fast that it was two steps ahead of her voice. She took a deep breath, forcing herself to think through her next series of commands before she gave them. "Lieutenant Alden, I want you to line the ship up with *both* Riley's and Tracey's coordinates."

"Aye, sir." The pilot's reply was confident enough, but the sidelong glance he gave her betrayed a little confusion. Uhura took a deep breath, realizing that this was the point at which she had to share her strategy with the rest of the crew, and see how they reacted to it.

"I don't want to engage the Shechenag ship in battle unless that's our very last resort," she said. "What we're going to do is obstruct their work so they can't finish their defensive network. It won't be anything fancy, like Commander Spock and Lieutenant Sulu did with the satellite network, but if we can place the Shechenag ship exactly in line between us and the Janus Gate, I think we can manage to disable her in a way that won't seem like it's coming from us. Can you keep the *Enterprise* on that station, Lieutenant Alden?"

"If I can't, sir, you better demote me to shuttle pilot," the helmsman replied resolutely, and Uhura felt the *Enterprise*'s impulse engines surge as she came around to her new heading.

The turbolift doors hissed open, and Lieutenant John Kyle strode onto the bridge. His bony face wore its usual deadpan expression, but the shrewd blue eyes were alert. "Lieutenant Kyle reporting to the bridge, sir. Do you need me to relieve the helm officer?"

"No, Lieutenant. I want you at engineering." Now that the critical part of her operation was at hand, Uhura found that she couldn't remain seated in the captain's chair no matter how hard she tried. She scrambled to her feet and went to join Kyle at the bridge's engineering station. Watkins, the on-duty engineer, was already vacating his station and heading for one of the auxiliary bridge monitoring stations so he could continue his work of coordinating bridge control with engine room response. "I want you to route the main transporter controls through here so we can aim and fire them like a weapon. The angle of the beam relative to the *Enterprise* may change, but the vector will always remain oriented toward the same spot on the planet's surface."

The transporter technician glanced down at the spatial coordinates that had been sent to the engineering station by Riley and Tracey. When he looked back up at Uhura, his pale eyebrows had curved into a distinctly dubious arc. "We're aiming the transporters at that Janus Gate area again?"

"Yes."

Kyle cleared his throat gingerly. "Forgive me for asking, Lieutenant, but have you cleared this with the chief? If we're going to risk losing all the ship's power, I think he'd like to know about it in advance."

Uhura frowned at the skeptical tone of Kyle's voice, but she knew better than to reprimand him. As one of the ship's main transporter technicians, he reported directly to Montgomery Scott, and right now he was just doing his duty as an engineer. She said over her shoulder to Hadley, "Contact Lieutenant Commander Scott in his quarters and tell him I need to clear a bridge operation with him." Then she glanced back up at Kyle. Her awareness of how fast time was running out for the landing party put a sharp edge in her voice that even she could hear. "While we wait, Lieutenant Kyle, I suggest you transfer controls and aim the transporter beam. You'll need to make sure it just grazes the edge of this first set of coordinates—" She pointed at the flickering column of spatial data that was Riley's fix on the slowly moving

Shechenag starship. "—then hits the Janus Gate as directly as possible."

"Aye-aye, sir." Whatever doubts he may have had, Kyle must have recognized from the intensity of Uhura's voice that there wasn't much leeway for delay. He seated himself at the engineering station and began programming it to take control of the main transporter beam, his long fingers not even hesitating over their work.

"I've got Lieutenant Commander Scott, sir." Lieutenant Hadley offered the frequency monitor to her, as if he'd already guessed that she'd prefer her conversation with Montgomery Scott to be semiprivate. As she crossed the bridge back to her old station, Uhura made a mental note to place a commendation for initiative in the young officer's personnel file. "He wants to know if you need him up on the bridge."

"I don't need you, sir," Uhura said into the transmitter. "I just need to clear a maneuver before I risk it."

"Whisht?" said a sleepy, Scottish voice in her ear. "I mean, what is it that you're wanting to do, lass?"

"The Shechenag are almost ready to place the last satellites in their defensive array. I have the *Enterprise* positioned so they're directly between us and the Janus Gate. I want to aim the main transporters to graze the Shechenag ship, as if we were trying to beam some of its hull down to the Janus Gate."

There was a short—and no longer sleepy—silence on the other end of the channel. "You're trying to get the Janus Gate to latch onto that alien ship and drain its power, the same way it bolluxed us up when we connected to it?"

"Yes, sir. Do I have your permission to try?"

The chief engineer blew out a gusty breath in her ear. "How much longer do we have before the shield closes up completely?"

Uhura glanced up at the planet on the viewscreen. Its opalescent glow was definitely brighter than before. "We're not sure, sir. Probably less than thirty minutes."

"And neither hide nor hair of Mr. Spock's shuttle to be seen?"

"No, sir."

This time, the sigh that echoed through the frequency monitor was much more resigned. "Then we'd better do something, hadn't we? Go ahead and try your maneuver, Lieutenant. You've got Kyle at the transporter controls, don't you?"

"Yes, sir."

"Good." In the distance, Uhura could hear the telltale hiss of a microfoam mattress decompacting as weight was removed from it. "Tell Kyle to shut the beam down at the first sign of a voltage fluctuation on the main access lines," Montgomery Scott ordered. "I'll head down to the engine room and make sure the warp core is shunted off from the ship's power circuits. Just in case the lad's aim with the transporter beam is as bad as his aim with darts," he added dryly. "Scott out."

Uhura handed the frequency monitor back to Hadley, and relayed the chief engineer's instructions to Kyle. He nodded, then added a few more lines of code to his rerouted transporter controls. "Do you want me to wait to make sure Commander Scott has time to get to the engine room?" he asked when he was done.

Uhura could hear the almost inaudible twitch of nervousness that lay beneath Kyle's question, probably because she was so nervous herself. Before she could be tempted to agree, she made herself turn and look up at Tlaoli. The dayside of the shielded planet was now a phosphorescent bone-white, while the nightside shimmered in the darkness of space like a drop of molten pearl.

"No," Uhura said sharply. "Mr. Alden, are we on station?"

"Right on station, sir."

"Mr. Riley, do we still have a precise fix on the Shechenag spaceship?"

"Down to one-tenth of a meter, sir."

Uhura would have liked to have taken a deep breath, but her abdominal muscles had locked so tight with tension that she couldn't manage it. She drew in a short, shallow breath instead, and hoped it didn't sound too much like a gasp. When she spoke, however, her voice didn't shake or quiver in the slightest. Uhura blessed her years of communications duty for that.

"Lieutenant Kyle, engage the transporter beam."

"Aye-aye, sir." The transporter technician's voice cracked with the tension Uhura had managed to hide, but to his credit he didn't hesitate. "Transporter beam engaged."

Unlike the phasers, there was no way to see the transporter beam shoot through space, and the lack of lights on the massive Shechenag starship made it hard to tell if any of its hull had been displaced by the beam. But Uhura knew the instant their beam hit the aliens' defensive shield. A bloom of fiery blue-white light erupted from the impact, then mushroomed across the opalescent surface, dissipating as it spread.

"What just happened, Mr. Kyle?" Uhura snapped.

The transporter technician tapped a query into his station desk. "It looks like the carrier wave never reached the planet, much less made a connection back for us to send anything along it." He threw a stymied look back over his shoulder at her. "Sir, our transporter beam just got completely absorbed by that defense shield out there."

# Chapter Nine

UHURA STARED UP AT Tlaoli on the viewscreen. Beyond the massive silhouette of the Shechenag starship, there was still a visible smudge of shadow on the fiery white crescent of the planet's dayside, marking the place where Spock and Sulu had blasted through the aliens' defensive array. But the repairs that had already been done to the satellite network had stitched enough of that hole closed to make it look more like a puckered seam than a puncture. And most of the remaining darkness lay far to starboard of the Shechenag's slow-moving ship.

"There's still enough of a gap left for the shuttle to come through," Uhura said, thinking out loud. "That means there should be enough space for us to shoot a transporter beam through, too."

"But we're not in the right place to make that angle, sir," Kyle pointed out. "We can line up the *Enterprise,* the Shechenag, and the Janus Gate, but that doesn't necessarily mean we'll be shooting through the widest part of—"

"I've got it calculated, sir," Riley broke in abruptly. "We need to be about a hundred kilometers closer to the planet and almost over its northern pole to make the shot."

"Then let's get there." Uhura seated herself back into the captain's chair in case the course correction was more than their inertial dampeners could easily handle. "Send those coordinates over to the helm, Mr. Riley. Estimated time of arrival, Mr. Alden?"

"I'm already headed for the general area, sir. It should only take a minute or two to re-establish our station." The pilot checked his screen, then frowned across at his navigator. "Do we really need to be *that* close to the thermosphere?"

"It's an oblique shot," Riley and Kyle said in unison.

Lieutenant Alden nodded, and Uhura felt the *Enterprise* shudder a little as it cut across Tlaoli's gravity well at a less than ideal vector. A moment later, another series of bumps shook through the bridge as they encountered a gravitational anomaly. That was a good sign, Uhura reminded herself as she clenched her fingers tighter around the armrests of the captain's chair. It meant they were approaching the area where the ancient planet's mysterious deviations in gravity hadn't been damped out by the Shechenag defensive shield.

"Estimated time of arrival now, Mr. Alden?" Uhura hoped her voice didn't sound as desperate as she felt. The shadowy gap in the satellite-generated force field was getting smaller even as they approached.

"One point five minutes, sir."

A warning alarm went off somewhere on the back of the bridge, and Uhura heard Watkins swing around at his auxiliary station. "We're scraping the planet's thermosphere, Lieutenant," the engineer warned. "The screens are holding so far, but if we stay here too long, the thermal gradient may cause them to fail."

"Be ready to shoot that transporter beam as soon as we've hit the correct location, Mr. Kyle," Uhura ordered. "Mr. Alden, get us on station *now.*"

"Aye, sir."

A minute was such a long time when you were balanced on the perilous edge of success and failure. Time for far too many quick, tense breaths, far too many thoughts of all the things that could go wrong...

"We're on station," Alden said.

"Coordinates of Shechenag ship updated and checked," Riley added in the same instant.

"Transporter beam locked and engaged," Kyle said, his voice overlapping the other two. "Beaming now."

There was another breathless pause, one in which Uhura forced herself not to spin around to watch the transporter technician at work. Instead, she stared at the dark, crawling shadow that was the Shechenag spaceship just below them. Nothing appeared to happen to its unlit hull, but nothing happened on the opalescent curve of the planet, either. Uhura waited as long as she could, then said, "Status report, Mr. Kyle?"

"That transporter beam went *somewhere,* sir," he said. "I got just a hint of return on the carrier wave, then it was gone, like we'd never sent it."

"Any power fluctuations?"

"None that I noticed."

"Sir!" Lieutenant Karen Tracey swung away from her science station. "I think something's happening to the Shechenag ship."

Uhura glanced up, but saw nothing obvious on the viewscreen. "What have you got?"

"My long-range scanners are picking up a lot of ionic discharge around their hull, but it's not contained or directed like an engine discharge would be. It's consistent with the signature of an unshielded ship falling into the planet's thermosphere."

"Or with them hitting their own defensive array?"

Tracey glanced down at her readings, then back up at Uhura with a little smile. "Yes, sir. It's consistent with that, too."

Uhura took a long, deep breath. It felt like her first in quite a while, and she heard it echoed in a soft chorus of relief around the bridge. "Congratulations, gentlemen," she said to her crew. "I think we've managed to stop the Shechenag from installing any more defensive satellites. All we have to do now is keep an eye on them in case they need a friendly lift to get out of their own force field." She looked back up at the silent white planet on the viewscreen, and felt a little of her triumph seep away. Tlaoli's dayside had nearly vanished from view, reminding Uhura that even if they kept an escape route open for their landing team, there were only a few hours left for them to use it. "And pray our shuttle returns while we still have time."

The explosion of light inside the Janus Gate took everyone by surprise. It didn't occur to Sulu until much later that he could easily have become part of that blast rather than merely part of its audience.

Ever since Sanner had returned from his marathon run and Spock had come out of his trance, the five remaining members of the landing party had been trying in vain to recharge the alien time transporter. A phaser blast from the ship had been their obvious first choice, but although the emergency communicator had been magnetically shielded to preserve its power, all it spat out at them when they tried to use it was a fierce crackle of static. Either the Janus Gate had just enough power left to disrupt any subspace transmissions that came near it, or, as Spock surmised, the Shechenag defensive shield around the planet was blocking all communicator frequencies.

After that, they tried powering the gate with whatever tools they had at hand. Yuki Smith discharged all of her phaser power cells by shooting her weapon directly into the device. The blue flame at its heart barely flickered in response. Sulu then suggested throwing their single photon grenade into it. Spock had vetoed that idea at first, but after they'd drained the power from all their other magnetically shielded instruments—including his own tricorder—with no apparent change in the Janus Gate, the Vulcan science officer reluctantly agreed to reconsider.

"We have no other energy reserves left, aside from the shuttle's warp core," Spock said thoughtfully. Although he moved a little more rigidly than usual, his voice had returned to its normal dispassionate tone. "We could allow the shuttle to crash on the surface above this chamber, but I am not certain that would allow for an efficient transfer of power into the Janus Gate. When the device's field strength is this low, its power-draining effects do not seem to extend far beyond this chamber."

Smith looked up from repacking her drained power cells and useless phaser rifle. They would have to resort to hand-to-hand combat if a Sheche-nag squadron attacked them now, Sulu thought. Of course, it might be worth it if they could toss the robotic aliens' power supplies into the gate when the fight was over.

"Is that why we could tromp around the cave for so long when we first came down here, sir, without noticing any problems in our instruments?" the security guard asked.

"Precisely the data point upon which I based my hypothesis, crewman," Spock said, and left Smith looking as if she wasn't quite sure what the answer to her question had been.

"Maybe that was why the ancient Tlaoli built their time transporter on a planet with gravitational anomalies," Zap Sanner speculated. "Once the planet made those ancient starships crash, then the Janus Gate could suck out their power."

Spock lifted one eyebrow at the cave geologist, but his comment wasn't the skeptical one Sulu expected. "You are assuming that the gravitational anomalies here are natural, Mr. Sanner. I am inclined to believe that the ancient Tlaoli may have actually created the instabilities themselves, perhaps by releasing a small singularity into the planet's metallic core—"

"Sir, the photon grenade," Chekov reminded him, although even as he spoke he looked a little alarmed by his own temerity in cutting through the scientists' discussion. "Do you think we should throw it into the gate?"

Spock paused, then gave the ensign a grave and reluctant nod. "Yes, I do. Endeavor to strike the center of the device, Mr. Chekov. We do not wish to damage the Janus Gate by hitting one of its outer arms—"

"Oh, no, you don't." Sulu intercepted Chekov before he could reach into Smith's pack of weaponry, extending himself with the same smooth lunge he used in fencing. "This was *my* idea. If the explosion gets thrown back from the gate, or makes one of those blue subspace rifts appear outside it, I'm going to be the one standing there, not you."

Chekov's dark eyes met his steadily. "But sir, I'm just—"

"—a member of this crew, like everybody else here," Sulu finished, cutting off whatever the younger man had meant to say. *I'm just an ensign? I'm just a new crewman, and more expendable than you?* Or maybe, *I'm just going to grow up to be someone bitter and hateful and I'd rather not do that?* In any case, it seemed even more important than usual to take the initiative on this particular plan. "Hand over that grenade to me, Mr. Smith."

The security guard paused for a moment, then carefully leaned around Chekov to give the small but powerful weapon to Sulu. "He gave me an order," she explained to the Russian. "And it *was* his idea."

Chekov looked frustrated and just a little rebellious. "At least let me come partway with you as backup," he said to Sulu stubbornly. The helmsman opened his mouth to say no, but saw the younger man's desperate need to be part of this rescue. It was almost as if he still blamed himself for that initial walk across the Janus chamber, when he'd inadvertently guided both Captain Kirk and himself into the time transporter's grasp.

"All right," Sulu said. "But you've got to stay at least a meter behind me."

"Yes, sir."

Sulu took a deep breath of air so warm and misty that it almost felt like he was back on Basaraba. Then he swung around and headed out into the Janus chamber with Chekov treading carefully one meter behind. Sulu glanced over at the curving metal arms of the device, and decided that the best place from which to toss the photon grenade would also be the safest place to stand: directly in front of the control station where Spock had stood to use the machine. That way, even if the grenade powered up the gate enough to create those drifting curtains of blue energy around it, Sulu—and Chekov behind him—would be standing inside the channel of protection the device made for its operator.

Sulu angled his carbide light down toward the ground, hoping to use the trace of Vulcan blood he'd seen before to lead him to the correct spot, but too much ice had melted since then. He had to rely on his memory instead, pausing once or twice to check his orientation against the Janus Gate, until he finally caught sight of the control panel Spock had used, and lined himself up with it. By then, Sulu could barely see the trio of glows that marked Spock, Sanner, and Smith watching them from across the cavern.

"I'm going to arm the grenade for time, not impact," he said over his shoulder to Chekov. "Just in case I miss getting it into the field generator."

"Good idea, sir. If it bounces back toward us, we'll have a chance to scoop it up and disarm it before it goes off."

Sulu snorted. "No, Mr. Chekov, we'll have a chance to run like hell. Are you ready?"

"Yes, sir."

Another deep breath of foggy air, and Sulu dug his fingers into the carefully recessed switch that activated the photon grenade's one minute timer. Then, with the same smooth movement he used to slide a riposte back under a fencing opponent's parry, he tossed the grenade up toward the Janus Gate. It sailed in a lazy arc directly toward the heart of flickering blue fire, erupting into a brilliant flash as soon as it hit the alien force field. Sulu hadn't expected the explosion to come before the timer triggered it—he jerked an arm up to shield his eyes, but it was too late to preserve the night sight he'd built up over hours of peering through the underground dimness. He kept his arm raised, waiting tensely for the shock wave that should have followed that explosion of powerful light, but not even a breath of wind hit his frostburned face. The Janus Gate must have absorbed the grenade's charge before it could convert its light to thermal and kinetic energy.

"Did it recharge?" Sulu lowered his arm and blinked at the alien device. It looked shadowy and blurred, but, then, so did everything else in his light-dazzled vision. He swung around to squint at the equally murky figure in the darkness behind him. "Mr. Chekov, can you tell if the grenade recharged the gate?"

Instead of answering, the younger man's silhouette took a step closer to Sulu. "Sir, are you all right?"

"I'm just light-blinded. *Did the gate recharge?"*

The pale blur that was Chekov's face shifted from an oval to a crescent as he glanced from Sulu to the alien device behind him. "I don't think—" he began, then sucked in a startled breath. Before Sulu could ask what was wrong, or turn his puzzled squint back toward the Janus Gate, a pair of gloved hands clamped onto his shoulders and yanked him forward with one desperate and violent pull. Chekov threw himself in the same direction, boots scrabbling against the wet cavern floor with such ferocity that even in his blinded state Sulu knew he should keep on going. He hit the cavern wall before he saw it, then staggered back a step and gasped for air. Chekov caught at his shoulder again and shoved him onward along the wall, toward the cave threshold where reaching arms caught him and reeled him into the narrow mouth of the conduit passage.

"What—?" Sulu's question was cut off by the tidal wave of light that crashed over all of them from behind. Unlike the brief, blinding flash of the photon grenade, this light was the blue of hot flame, and it didn't die away. Instead it grew and grew, until the whole passage glowed with arc-discharge intensity. Sulu covered even his already blinded eyes, feeling tears of pain roll out from beneath his tightly closed eyelids as the light burned against them. He could feel the wave of intense cold that came after it, and hear the sudden fierce crackle as meltwater turned abruptly back to ice inside the chamber. The temperature-sensitive fibers of his caving suit swelled so fast he could feel the cloth ripple against his skin.

"Did I do that?" he asked when the fiercest part of the light-storm had passed. The other members of the cave team were all blinking and squinting as badly as he was in the blue radiance that bathed them, but Spock managed to get an eyebrow up in spite of that.

"Unlikely," the Vulcan said. "There was too much elapsed time between your grenade explosion and the Janus Gate's response." He eyed the blue glow, which had subsided now to the same kind of rippling light-waves they'd seen before. "This much power can only have come from the *Enterprise.* She either speculated correctly that we were in need of assistance—or she found it necessary to punch another hole in the Shechenag defensive array."

"Does that mean the Shechenag might have closed up our first exit hole?" Sanner asked. Sulu's vision was returning, and he could see the way Smith's and Chekov's faces both tightened at that suggestion. If Sanner was right, and they didn't get Captain Kirk back soon, they might find themselves trapped forever on this small, dead planet.

"You said you had another way to retrieve the captain," Sulu said to Spock. "Let's do it, now, before anything else happens to interfere."

"Very well," Spock said, and reached for him.

Kirk heard the horrible *smack!* of a high-speed projectile slamming into a human body as he threw himself to the floor, followed almost immediately by

George's startled shout of alarm and the muffled thud of someone falling as a dead weight.

*Not the boy! Please, God, don't let them hit the boy!*

But he could hear the boy reassuring someone who'd called to him, in a startlingly calm voice for all that the pitch betrayed his fear. Kirk wedged himself into the corner made by the barricade and the corridor wall, his phaser close across his chest, and took stock of who'd been hit and how badly even as another fusillade of shots pummeled the front of the barricade.

Sulu crouched across the corridor from Kirk, carefully fitting the muzzle of his rifle between the edge of one crate and the wall so he could return fire. Back toward the bay door, George Kirk had his son pinned flat to the floor, shielding the boy with his own body while Chekov scrabbled to overturn the grav-sled between them and the attackers outside. The Russian's right hand left a splayed, bloody print wherever it touched, but whatever injury he'd taken didn't seem to slow him and Kirk couldn't worry about anyone who was still in a position to take care of himself. It was Giotto who had spilled the majority of the blood in the corridor. The security chief lay spread-eagled in the largest puddle, eyes fixed blindly up at the ceiling, not moving.

"Commander Kirk!" Kirk scrambled forward on hands and knees to grab Giotto's belt and drag him to a more protected location. "Keep working on that door! It's our only way out now."

Keeping his son close to his side, George edged back toward the big door a few feet at a time, hauling the grav-sled along behind them as a kind of portable shield. "I'll need his phaser," he called, to no one in particular, and Chekov darted to scoop up Giotto's abandoned weapon and underhand it to George's son on his way to Sulu's side of their beleaguered wall of crates.

The shooting outside paused, and Kirk wondered if their attackers actually had to stop and reload, or if they'd gone in search of more powerful weapons. He hauled Giotto mostly upright by the front of his cave jumper, ignoring the chief's shuddering gasp of pain as he propped him up against the corridor wall. Kirk had heard something once about keeping victims of chest wounds upright to prevent them from drowning in their own blood. He had no idea if this was true, but didn't know what else he could do for the man.

"How is he?"

Kirk spared Chekov only a glance, just long enough to see the look of bleak concern on his face as he submitted to Sulu's businesslike inspection of his own bleeding arm, and that he was in no immediate danger of dying. Still, the raw desperation in his eyes bothered Kirk more than he cared to admit. Kirk turned back to Giotto with a grim shake of his head. "Not good." He was still breathing, but even that sounded tenuous and fluid.

"Believe it or not, Captain, that might actually be a good thing." Sulu finished his examination and wiped both hands on the front of his jumper to clear them of blood. "It passed straight through," he told Chekov, picking up his own rifle again.

Chekov scowled with unconcealed anger. "I know it went through. How do you think Giotto got hit?"

Watching him snap the control on his rifle over to its multishot function, Kirk realized that Chekov was more angry at himself than at their attackers, as though he'd failed in some important duty by not stopping the projectile himself. He'd be a hard subordinate to keep alive for any length of time. Kirk wondered if this was a problem he was bound to face with the young man he'd left back on board the *Enterprise,* too, or if there was something about their unmentioned alternate future to blame.

As Chekov lifted the rifle over the top of the barricade to fire a blind salvo down the hall, Kirk asked Sulu, "Can you see anything from where you are?"

The other captain leaned to put one eye to the small crack he'd managed to insinuate between the crates. "Six gunmen, all natives." He waited through the next round of gunfire. "I don't think they have energy weapons, just projectiles."

That was one advantage. "Either unskilled workers or an advance guard," Kirk guessed. He followed Chekov's example and aimed a single phaser shot over the edge of the barricade on wide-dispersal stun. Native voices shouted in a mixture of anger and alarm, but Kirk heard the clatter of their retreat a few meters farther down the hall. "Now let's hope we can get that door open before one of them thinks to drag in an Orion pulse cannon."

"If we're here that long, we have more problems than just that door." Chekov raised up just high enough to glance over the rim of their barricade, squeezed off a shot at whatever he saw, then dropped back down to floor level again. He turned a furious glare on Sulu. "Where is he?"

The other captain remained calmly attentive to his spy hole. "Give it a minute."

"Why?" Chekov demanded. "They're twenty years in the future, dammit! They could put him in the device *six weeks* after we left, and he should still arrive the moment the man went down!"

Kirk followed the angry gesture thrown in his direction, and realized with a jolt that the "man" Chekov referred to was Giotto. He tightened his hand protectively on the security chief's shoulder. "Is this what you meant when you said Giotto was linked back to the device? That it would somehow replace him if he died?"

"No, that wasn't our plan." Sulu sat back from the barricade with a sigh, rubbing at his right wrist as though it pained him. "But that's something like how the device works. As long as you're healthy, it takes whatever version of you steps into the machine and uses that version to replace a damaged version of you from somewhere else in your timeline."

"Which means the younger version of him we lifted out when we came here should have shown up by now." Chekov's face was drawn with anxiety, and Kirk had a feeling there was more at stake in Giotto's failure to appear than was obvious to him at the moment.

"We're in!"

George's shout rang out just ahead of the bay door's loud exhalation, and the hatch rolled aside with a tremendous rumbling that made their metal crate barricade shiver and spread at the seams. Kirk lunged forward to steady the segment closest to him, and saw two of the Vragax outside break from their own cover to flee down the corridor back the way they'd come. He had a feeling that the Orions and whatever heavy weapons they still had at their disposal wouldn't be long in coming.

Shouldering up beside Chekov, Kirk slapped Sulu on the shoulder and motioned toward Giotto. "Get him inside the bay and loaded on board our transport. Chekov and I will cover you."

The older captain nodded, but it was a boy's voice that said, dismally, "There's only one seat."

Kirk twisted a look back over his shoulder, meeting his own eyes in the doorway even as a projectile burned past his ear so close that he heard the buzz of its passage. The boy was on his knees, as protected as possible, craning around the edge of the bulkhead with his eyes wide and hollow with despair. "It's a personal escape craft." Kirk knew he was trying to sound adult and brave, but he was too close to tears to be convincing. "There's only one seat. My dad says I can fit under the panel while he flies, but—"

"Go!" Kirk told him. Nothing else the boy had to say mattered.

"I'm not leaving you!"

*This isn't the shuttle!* Kirk wanted to shout at him. *I'm not Maione!* But he knew the boy wouldn't understand, not for another nineteen years.

Instead, it was Chekov who said, "Don't worry about us. We have our own escape route."

It occurred to Kirk that his young ensign was going to evolve into a rather accomplished liar.

"But I heard you," the boy protested, his hands clenching and unclenching on the bloodied floor. "Mr. Giotto isn't coming."

Chekov cracked open his rifle to expel a jammed projectile from the barrel. "Mr. Giotto was Plan A." He sounded much calmer than before, but his face was still grim and pale. "We still have Plan B."

The boy said nothing for a moment, and Kirk heard his father call, "Jimmy! We have to go, son!" from somewhere farther back in the shuttlebay. Instead of answering that shout, the boy asked, very quietly, "You really have a Plan B? You're not just lying to me."

For the first time, Chekov turned to look at him, and the sincerity in his expression made Kirk both angry and glad. "I wouldn't lie to you," the older man said, taking advantage of the strange, earnest trust in the boy's eyes in a way that made clear to Kirk he hadn't been the one to earn it in the first place. "We have a Plan B. Now go with your father."

The boy hesitated for another long, painful moment. Then, just before Kirk would have broken from the others to drag his younger self into the bay, the boy backed away from the doorway and let it roll shut behind him with a boom like distant thunder. As though that final sound were some sort of signal only he could understand, Chekov turned stonily back to the barricade, and away from their last chance of escaping Grex alive.

Kirk watched him reassemble his rifle and switch it back to single rate-of-fire. "I don't suppose we have something more than a good lie to fall back on."

The shuttle's launch roared through the corridor, toppling metal crates both across their barricade and around their Vragax attackers down the hall. "I didn't lie," Chekov said, charging the gauss rifle's barrel until the whole gun began to hum. "We really do have a Plan B." He looked up at Sulu, and Kirk saw the silent communication that passed between them even though he didn't know the language.

But he recognized the shocked disbelief on the other captain's face an instant before Chekov swung the rifle toward Sulu—and fired.

For a moment, Sulu thought the Vulcan was intending to use him as a support because he no longer had enough strength to walk back out to the Janus Gate by himself. But when Spock's fingers tightened around his shoulder like a vise and steered him toward the blue-lit chamber with irresistible Vulcan strength, Sulu realized he was going to be used for something more than just a crutch. A jolt of shock went through him when he realized Spock was guiding him toward the far side of the time transporter, where Giotto had stood—and then vanished—just a short while before.

"You don't need to push me, Commander," Sulu said. The words were prosaic enough, but he hoped they would convey his determination to carry out whatever obligation his duty as a Starfleet officer required. "I can see well enough to walk out on my own."

The Vulcan science officer relaxed the intensity of his grip, but did not let go of Sulu's shoulder. "You have never approached this part of the device, Lieutenant," he replied calmly. "With the amount of power in the Janus Gate now, the protected area leading to it has undoubtedly narrowed."

Sulu blinked and swung his head back and forth so he could use the more light-sensitive edges of his vision. "I see it." Ribbons of intense blue fire twisted and burned on either side of the chamber, but a channel of clear air kept them from meeting each other. "I can get there from here, Commander."

His voice must have carried his willingness clearly enough for even a Vulcan to comprehend. Spock removed his hand from Sulu's shoulder. "I believe I will be able to send you directly to Captain Kirk on our first attempt, but if you see Basaraba instead, tell me immediately. And whatever happens, Mr. Sulu, do not release those supports."

Sulu followed his gaze to the oddly curved attachments projecting out from this side of the alien time transporter and felt his fingers curl involuntarily, as if to memorize the muscle motion he would need to keep himself linked to Tlaoli and the present. "Aye, sir," he said, and started down the evanescent path toward the roiling blue fireball that was the Janus Gate.

Despite his stiffness, Spock moved back around the edge of the chamber quickly enough that he was already in place by the time Sulu had summoned up the will to place his hands on the black metal supports. Runnels of liquid blue light already crawled along the arms that enclosed the gate's subspace field generator, only a few centimeters away from his fingers. Sulu forced himself to stand still as those streaks of light spiraled toward him.

"I have set the machine for viewing mode," Spock said calmly. Sulu nodded, trying not to think of what had happened the last time they had tried to use the Janus Gate to peer into the past. It didn't seem as if the room was quite as bright now as it had been then, but there was no guarantee the *Enterprise* wouldn't send another phaser shot or transporter beam down at any moment, adding more energy to the alien power storage system. "This should take you directly to—"

Sulu gasped, then nearly choked on the intense bite of cold air inside his unwary throat. There had been no warning, just an instant of disorientation and a sense of sudden jarring—then he was standing somewhere completely different. An echoing space like a corridor or a shuttlebay, brightly lit by red-tinged photon lamps and echoing with the *spang* and *whirr* of projectile fire. Sulu glanced around, finding himself just barely able to swing his head and completely unable to move aside from that.

"This definitely isn't Basaraba," he informed a Spock he could no longer see, and saw an abrupt jerk of motion off to one side, as if someone else had heard and recognized his voice.

"*Sulu!* Here!"

He knew that harsh Russian-accented voice, although it grated now in a painful way it had never done before, even in their most desperate moments together on Basaraba. Sulu clenched his hands around the cold metal supports he could still feel back on Tlaoli, and with an enormous effort slewed himself around to look in that direction. He could see two faces swing up to stare at him from behind what looked like a tumble of battered metal crates. Gunfire still blazed out across the room behind them, but neither man was shooting back at their attackers. Instead, it looked as if they were huddled over two fallen comrades—one propped awkwardly against the corridor wall, the other cradled inside Chekov's bloodstained arms.

*"Go!"* the older Russian said, his voice cutting like a ragged knife through the clatter of weapons fire. "Take Giotto and *go!"*

The other crouching man rocked back on his heels. "You knew he'd come," he said, in a voice Sulu recognized even when it sounded as shocked and exhausted as this. "It's because of the way the time machine works—"

"That you're going to be able to get back to where you should be, and erase everything that has happened in my lifetime!" Chekov reached out with a long black rifle, but all he did with it was shove Kirk farther away from him. "Now *go!*"

The captain scrambled to his feet and turned to heave Giotto upright, in preparation for hefting him in a fireman's carry. Sulu heard the security chief groan in pain, and with another surge of sheer willpower managed to pull himself closer to both men.

"Mr. Spock, I have them! I have Captain Kirk and Commander Giotto." Sulu almost reached out with his real hands, but caught himself just before his fingers slipped off the cold metal arms of the Janus Gate. This required a mental effort, not a physical one. He felt his teeth dig into his lip, felt blood drip and then freeze against his face as he forced himself to stretch the disembodied shadows of what would have been arms if he had really been present in this timeline. Something as sharp and unpleasant as an electric shock jolted through him. A flash of eerie blue light leaped out from where Sulu seemed to stand and connected with Giotto. An instant later, the security chief was gone.

Sulu heard a distant sound of startled shrieks and wails of fear, and the gunfire stopped abruptly. In the ringing silence that followed, he could hear Chekov whispering, over and over again, "...I'm sorry...I'm so sorry..."

Kirk threw one last glance over his shoulder, and in the blue light that Sulu realized must be coming from himself, he saw compassion blossom on the captain's face. "He knew—" he said softly. But before he could complete the sentence, another electric jolt shuddered through Sulu, and Kirk disappeared as well.

But something still connected Sulu himself to this past he'd never lived through. He squinted through the sterile glare of reddish light, not at Chekov, but at the slumped figure in his protective grasp. There was no way to see the dead man's face, turned as it was into his first officer's bloodstained shoulder, but Sulu recognized that wiry build. He saw it in the mirror every day.

"You shot him." It wasn't an accusation so much as a belated realization, an understanding of how Spock had managed to send him to a place he'd never been. The glare Chekov gave him scorched his face with embarrassment. Sulu suddenly knew what Kirk had been trying to tell the older Russian. "I know you only did it to get me here. He must have known, too—"

"He didn't know anything." The older man's voice had thickened to a barely recognizable mutter. "Except that he was going to die—"

"To keep the Gorn invasion from happening," Sulu insisted. "And you know he would have wanted—"

He broke off, because it was clear his words weren't needed anymore. Chekov had lifted his head, an odd, arrested expression chasing the pain out of his eyes for the first time Sulu could remember. "Do you hear that?" he asked softly.

But before Sulu could reply, the Russian officer's crouched figure, and that of his crumpled captain, rippled once as if a wind had blown through them, then faded into darkness and were gone.

# Chapter Ten

ONE MILKY THREAD at a time, the alien ship spun its slow cocoon around the blurry red disk that was Tlaoli. Kirk had started out counting each of the tiny satellites as the big ship placed them, but soon lost track as the white cataract they constructed grew too bright and dense. Now, the black surface of the ship stood in stark silhouette against that glowing backdrop. Soon, the alien protection sphere would be complete, and not even a hint of the planet's russet surface would be visible then. Only the Shechenag knew what would happen after that.

*Enterprise* had towed the big ship out of the planet's thermosphere the moment the shuttle cleared the satellite field. They'd deposited the Shechenag safely beyond the range of the Janus Gate's power-draining effect, even though Spock believed the device was too low on power now to reach beyond its own atmosphere in search of more. Kirk tried to explain the concept "Better safe than sorry," but only earned himself a stoic Vulcan lecture on the illogic of making decisions based on statistically unlikely outcomes.

It took the Shechenag less than four hours to reinstate power and return to their self-appointed task. They'd answered no hails in that time, and sent out no signals that Uhura could detect. They might have been any other soulless force of nature for all that they seemed interested in discussing their mission with the humans or finding out how the final activation of the Janus Gate had been resolved. Maybe they already knew. Kirk felt a strange guilt at having caused such vast upset and disruption for another race, like a child whose innocent game of catch inadvertently destroyed a priceless stained glass window. He caught himself wishing he could somehow go back and prevent any of it from happening.

*But that's how we got here in the first place.*

"You sent for me, Captain."

Kirk drew his attention away from Tlaoli's slowly accreting shroud, back to this dark observation deck and the officer who'd just entered it behind him. Spock's reflection in the transparent aluminum window gazed back at him with the same cool patience Kirk had been trying to get used to ever since promoting the Vulcan after Gary Mitchell's death. He remembered the pain he'd seen on that face only a few days before, when the Psi 2000 virus uncovered a cache of buried emotion so raw it would humiliate even the sternest Vulcan. And he wondered which Spock was the one he'd begun to let into his confidence—the one who admitted to loving his human mother, or the one he was afraid stood behind him now.

He turned his focus back outward toward the Shechenag ship. "Yes, Mr. Spock, I did." Two more satellites drifted neatly into place while he struggled with how to approach what was bothering him. "I've been thinking about the events leading up to my . . . retrieval from the past," he said at last.

Spock nodded as he stepped closer to the long window and joined Kirk in studying the alien construction. "And certain—" He paused to choose his words, and the unexpected show of consideration irritated Kirk. "—emotionally charged aspects of the events disturb you."

"You knew." He hadn't wanted to sound accusatory, but found he couldn't hide his anger and disappointment despite his best intentions. "After Giotto was accidentally transported, there was no way to reestablish a link to Grex without using someone who was already there." He looked at the Vulcan bluntly. "You knew Chekov was going to kill Sulu to make that link available."

"Indeed." Kirk knew it was irrational to expect remorse in the Vulcan's tone, but he still found himself wanting something more than mere logical acceptance of what had happened. When Spock gave it to him, however, it was in a very different form than he'd imagined. "Commander Chekov informed me of his intentions before the transfer was attempted."

Kirk swallowed around the sudden unpleasant lurch in his stomach. He thought he'd been prepared for where this conversation would take them—into the unsavory reality of his alien first officer convincing a subordinate human to do something unthinkably merciless. It had never occurred to him that the human involved had actually volunteered for the task.

"When we returned to the Janus Gate against the Shechenag's wishes," Spock continued, "I calculated a significant probability that they would endeavor to regain control over the gate and, in so doing, interrupt Mr. Giotto's contact with the device. If that occurred and Mr. Giotto was rendered unconscious or even killed, there would have been no other way to reestablish our link to Grex. It was an unfortunate weakness in our plan, and one which Commander Chekov identified without input from me." He seemed to consider for a moment whether or not to go on. "Unfortunately, we had already determined that certain aspects of Commander Chekov's personality made it impossible to use him as a focal point for the device. Our only recourse was to utilize Captain Sulu in that capacity. And in order for the device to work properly, Captain Sulu could not be informed of that in advance."

Kirk didn't know which part of the solution seemed most cruel, being the man who didn't know how his life was going to end, or being the man who knew he was going to end it.

"You must understand," Spock said, with a gentleness Kirk didn't think he'd ever heard in that voice before. "Captain Sulu and Commander Chekov were fully aware that your retrieval would result in the negation of the timeline representing the world they knew. Rescuing you from the past meant the end of their existence, regardless of how it was accomplished." When Kirk said nothing in response, the Vulcan reached out and touched him lightly on the sleeve. "Jim, it was a future they would have done anything to prevent."

*And one of them did.*

"But what if this wasn't enough?" He looked up at his first officer, his hands curling tight around the rail at his waist. "What if *I'm* not enough? Spock, a man killed his best friend because he believed I could change the world. Is any one person really that important?"

One of the things he valued most about Spock was that he earnestly considered any question you asked him, no matter how unanswerable. "One person," the Vulcan said at last, "perhaps not. But one event can change the course of history. And in the future they remembered, it was a single encounter with the Gorn which laid the foundation for the Federation's destruction." He met Kirk's gaze without flinching. "As captain of the *Enterprise,* you will be the man who determines the outcome of that encounter."

Kirk wasn't sure he found that reassuring. He tried

to imagine Gary Mitchell as a starship commander—straightforward, hotheaded Gary Mitchell. He'd been a good man at heart, but Kirk also knew that Gary hadn't been the sort of man to think about things too deeply. He didn't doubt for a moment that Gary would kill an alien starship commander if he believed it was the only way to save his crew. But would Kirk really do anything so very different? Short of sacrificing his own ship and crew, what other choices would he have?

Kirk stared out at the Shechenag and their nearly completed array, although they weren't the aliens he was thinking about. "So when we meet the Gorn at this planet called Cestus Three, all I have to do is figure out how not to irritate the Metrons—or, failing that, how to keep the Gorn commander alive when he's doing his best to kill me." He angled a wry grin up at Spock. "And I'll have to do it all with no memory of anything we found out here, won't I? With no idea what it means to the Federation if I fail."

The Vulcan actually seemed a little flustered by the question. "I cannot answer that with any certainty."

No data, of course. No other starship had been flung backward in time, then had to wait for the timeline to heal itself just to find out what they would or wouldn't remember. Or maybe they had, and the lack of evidence only served to prove Kirk's suspicions.

"Maybe it's better if we don't remember," he said aloud, letting his science officer off the hook both in relation to his question and the horrible events that had returned him to the *Enterprise.* "Maybe it isn't good to know too much about the consequences of the decisions we make." He tried on a resigned smile that probably looked as inauthentic as it felt. "Thank you, Mr. Spock. You're dismissed."

Spock merely lifted one eyebrow and dipped his own head in return. "You are welcome, Captain." Then he backed gracefully to the door, and let himself out.

Kirk watched him leave, wondering if humans were as incomprehensible to Vulcans as Vulcans sometimes seemed to him. And wondering if Vulcans valued the friendships possible in such combinations, or merely viewed them as the unavoidable byproduct of close association.

*I have to be fair to the Gorn.* He watched the Shechenag place the last link in their network, saw the gleaming cataract obscuring Tlaoli swell brighter and brighter. *If I remember nothing else about these three days, I have to somehow remember that.* He didn't know who the Gorn were, or what they looked like, or how he could possibly alter the course of a future so terrible that men would kill people they loved in an effort to avoid it. But as the brilliant shell around Tlaoli spilled over into complete invisibility, he realized that there would be nothing here to see or find, nothing outside himself to remind him. It really would all come down to him, and how he responded to a single alien commander when he thought all other choices were gone.

*I have to be fair to the Gorn. No matter what happens, I have to be fair—*

It was odd, Uhura reflected, but it felt as if it had been a long time since she'd been able to go to the rec room and eat a normal, leisurely meal.

She took her time at the menu panel, finally selecting a type of Basque seafood crepe that she had never tried before and a chocolate-hazelnut croissant for dessert. Then she spent almost as long deciding which kind of tea would best complement her dinner. It felt like a luxury just to be able to think about things as trivial as food, although if Uhura really cast her mind back, she couldn't remember anything much more important happening during the past few days. Still, there was no telling what urgent mission the *Enterprise* might be sent on now that their three-day jaunt into the past had come to an end and they were resuming normal Starfleet duties. She decided to just enjoy the sense of tranquility while it lasted and not worry about the future.

As she paused to stir honey into her pot of silverthread tea, Uhura noticed a young security guard fidgeting indecisively at the edge of the eating area, her own supper tray tucked under one arm. The young woman's frank and cheerful face sparked a vague memory of having met her on some past landing party or other, and as she came up beside her, Uhura gave her a friendly nod of greeting.

"Waiting for a table to open?" she asked, conversationally.

"Uh...no, Lieutenant. Not exactly." The security guard looked a little abashed, but only a little. "There's a guy sitting all by himself over there," she confided. "I was thinking I'd go sit with him, because I'm really sure I met him once, but I can't remember his name."

Uhura followed the direction of her glance to where a dark-haired young command ensign sat alone at the end of one table, gazing rather disconsolately down at his plate. "Oh, I know him," she said. "Come on. I'll pretend to introduce you and then if it turns out that he already knows you, we can all laugh about it."

"All right." The young woman followed her readily enough through the maze of tables. "My name's Yuki Smith, sir. Just in case you weren't sure."

Uhura tossed a smile back over her shoulder. "I think I knew that...but it never hurts to remind a senior officer who you are when you're new on board."

"That's for sure," Smith agreed. "I could have sworn Chief Giotto had me slated for the next landing party that went out, but he must have mixed me up with someone else, because the roster came out today and I'm on ship duty for the next three missions."

The dark-haired ensign looked up in surprise when they halted beside him, pushing his chair back and starting to rise despite the fact that it looked as if he'd barely touched his dinner. "Do you need this table, sir? I can move—"

"But then we'd just have to follow you," Uhura

replied, then laughed as his surprised look turned into something closer to alarm. "I came over to introduce you to someone I thought you'd like to meet. Yuki Smith, this is—"

She hadn't realized, right up to the very second that she was about to say his name, that she didn't actually know it. Of course, she knew it. For some reason it had just slipped off the tip of her tongue, the way words could do when you were very tired and sleepy. Although after three uneventful days of rest and recuperation from the Psi 2000 virus, right now Uhura didn't even have that excuse to justify her inexplicable lapse.

Her training as a professional communications officer stood her in good stead, however. "I'm sorry," she said to the young man, as gracefully as she would have apologized if she'd mistakenly used an Orion frequency to hail an Andorian vessel. "I know I should remember your name, but I just—forgot it."

"It's Chekov, sir. Pavel Chekov." His Russian accent seemed familiar, and he returned Yuki Smith's nod of greeting as if she were someone he already knew, but he eyed Uhura with real puzzlement. "I'm not sure why you should remember me, sir. I'm new on board, and I haven't done a turn at communications duty."

"Yet," Uhura said, seating herself at the table with her supper. The more she thought about it, the less able she was to pin down why she'd been so sure she knew this young man. But even if she didn't, it never hurt to let junior officers think that their seniors were keeping track of them at all times.

A smiling Yuki Smith took the chair opposite Chekov and pointed at his dinner. "What's that you're eating? It looks interesting."

"I'm not sure." The young Russian glanced down at the spongy round of pan bread with its colorful heaps of pureed legumes and stewed meats. "It seemed like something I should try...but now I'm not sure what parts of it are safe to eat."

"Northern African stews can be pretty spicy," Uhura agreed, as she dug into her seafood crepe. "I'd watch out for the red ones, if I were you. The yellow ones are probably milder."

"How *much* milder?" he asked worriedly.

"Here, I can taste it for you and let you know if it's okay." Smith stuck the tip of her fork into one of the yellow stews and lifted a morsel to her lips. A moment later, her cheerful face turned bright red and she reached abruptly for her water glass. "*Wow.* If that's mild, I'd hate to taste the hot ones."

"Yes." Chekov regarded his meal gloomily. "That's what I was afraid of."

A fourth chair squeaked against the decking, and Uhura glanced up to see Sulu plunk himself next to Chekov with all the familiarity of an old friend. "Hey," the pilot said. "What's good for dinner?"

"*Not* the North African platter," Yuki Smith advised him. "Unless you're really mad at the roof of your mouth. Sir," the security guard added belatedly, as if she'd just noticed his rank.

Sulu glanced from her to Chekov, then across the

table at Uhura. She saw the same sudden lack of certainty in his dark eyes that she'd felt a moment before and took pity on him. "Lieutenant Sulu, I think you know Pavel Chekov and Yuki Smith."

"I think so, too." Was it Uhura's imagination, or did Sulu sound just the slightest bit puzzled by that fact. "Aren't you going to eat any of that food, Chekov?"

"No, sir." An unexpected glint of humor flashed in the younger man's eyes. "I'm just trying to decide whether to take it to the food disposal chute or a hazardous waste port."

"Here, give it to me." Sulu ripped off an edge of the spongy bread and scooped up some of the darkest red stew, making both Chekov and Smith wince in anticipation. But the pilot's complexion never changed as he ate it. "So," he said to Uhura around another mouthful. "I hear you're having a dinner party for Riley?"

She nodded. "To make him feel a little better, after what happened back at Psi 2000."

"I assume I'm invited since I made an idiot of myself back there, too. Who else is coming?"

Uhura glanced across the mess hall to where the ordinance and weapons officers had gathered for their meal. Two of them sat a small but significant space apart from the others. "Well, I *was* going to invite Angela Martine and Robbie Tomlinson, but apparently they have other plans."

Sulu followed her gaze, his eyebrows lifting. "Huh. Since when have those two been an item?"

"I'm not sure," Uhura admitted. "I hope they don't

get in trouble for dating within the same department... but they do make a cute couple." Her eyes fell on a closer couple, one of whom was shyly offering the other half of her sandwich. "Are you two free for dinner tomorrow night?"

Chekov choked on his first bite, and Sulu had to lean over to thump the ensign between the shoulder blades before he could answer. While she was waiting, Uhura heard the scientific discussion at the table next to theirs rise to a heated pitch.

"—theoretically possible, Zap, but why are you even worrying about it?" said an exasperated Germanic voice. "I've never heard of any caves with those kinds of thermal gradients."

"Well, geez, Jaeger, we're on a five-year, deep-space mission here. You don't think we might run into *some* kind of cave we've never seen before while we're out here?"

"I'm sure we will. But I'm not going to waste *my* time trying to balance a thermodynamic equation for something that might not even exist. And even if it did, this ridiculous notion of endothermic energy storage—"

"I don't know if I *can* come to your dinner party, sir," Chekov said, when he'd finally regained his breath. "I mean... I think I'm scheduled for a second-shift turn in astrophysics."

"I know Lieutenant Boma pretty well," Uhura assured him. "I think I can arrange a change in shift for you. Can you come, too, Yuki?"

"I sure can. Thanks, Lieutenant." The security guard caught sight of the wall chronometer and made a dismayed noise. "Speaking of shifts, I'm going to be late for mine in another minute. You can have the rest of my fries, too, Pavel. See you guys tomorrow!"

They waved her good-bye, then finished their meals in an oddly companionable silence. "I'm headed down for the gym," Sulu said, as he rolled up the last rag of bread and popped it into his mouth. "You want to come along, Chekov?"

The Russian gave him a worried look. "You're not going to practice fencing, are you, sir?"

"Not for a long time," Sulu assured him emphatically. "I was just going to use the weights and punching bags." He rose to his feet and gave the younger man a friendly tap on the shoulder. "Who knows, you might get lucky and have Captain Kirk ask you to be his sparring partner. It's always good to catch the captain's eye when you're one of the new scuts on board. Otherwise you'll never get picked for a landing party."

"Knocking me down might make the captain remember me," Chekov agreed, following Sulu toward the door. "But I don't think it will get me any closer to a landing party. In fact, if I was the captain—"

Uhura finished the rest of her croissant in quiet and happy tranquility. The best part about serving on the *Enterprise,* she thought, was having so many good crewmates to work with that you were always meeting new ones even years into the mission. And wasn't it interesting how it sometimes seemed as if you had known them all along...

"I'm glad someone's happy around here," said McCoy's amused voice behind her, and Uhura realized with a little start of embarrassment that she had been humming one of her favorite songs beneath her breath. "If you listened to Spock, you'd think the entire galaxy was coming to an end."

Uhura scooted aside politely to let the ship's doctor and chief science officer sit down with their own dinners. It was typical of them, she thought, to share a meal even as they argued through one of their philosophical disagreements.

"I made no such statement, Doctor," said the Vulcan, calmly. "I merely pointed out that we have no logical way of knowing if our three-day journey into the past had any permanent effects on our future."

"Well, I don't feel any different than I did before we left Psi 2000," McCoy retorted. "Do you, Lieutenant?"

Uhura considered that question for a moment. "A little more tired," she decided, and saw the concerned look Dr. McCoy gave her. "I know, report to sickbay for a checkup," she said before he could. "I will, sir, but I think it's just the work we've all been doing. The last three days went past in such a blur..."

"My point, precisely," said Spock. "No one on the crew seems to have very clear memories of what we spent the last three days doing. I can only conclude that we have somehow merged with or been overlain by the versions of ourselves which already existed in the timeline before we returned to it, whose memories do not include the duplicated period of time."

"That doesn't sound very logical to me," McCoy retorted. "That other version of the *Enterprise* went to Psi 2000 and then got thrown back in time. It didn't stick around to merge with us."

"Not in our original timeline," Spock agreed. "But if we created changes in the timeline while we were duplicating ourselves, it is possible that we altered our own future enough to slide into a parallel timestream where we did not go to Psi 2000—"

"Not according to my medical records, which still show that I had to give viral antitoxin to about two hundred crewmen infected with the Psi 2000 virus!" The doctor pointed across the table with his fork. "Face it, Spock. This is all just wishful thinking, because you want to have been right about the dangers of going back in time."

The science officer arched a disdainful eyebrow. "Unlike you, Doctor, I do not attach emotional desires to my scientific hypotheses. I am merely attempting to explain certain anomalies that I have observed in the memories of the crew since we have returned to our proper place in time."

"I don't have any logical rationale for saying this, Mr. Spock," Uhura said quietly. "But if we *did* alter the timeline when we were back in the past…I have a feeling that we did it for the better."

"Me, too." McCoy waved his fork as if it were a

triumphal flag. "That's two votes to your one, Spock. We win."

The Vulcan looked pained. "That is the most illogical way of confirming a hypothesis that I have ever heard you use, Doctor. And I have heard you use quite a few completely illogical thought processes..."

"It's just as logical as saying that we've slipped into some different timestream that nobody knows is different. What about that favorite saying of yours, Spock: a difference that makes no difference is no difference? Doesn't that apply here?"

"Indeed, Doctor, but you have not yet convinced me that there is no difference. If you had taken the time to examine the evidence before you made up your mind, rather than afterward—"

Uhura slid out of her seat and headed for the rec room door, smiling as she heard the familiar debate roll on without her. Mr. Spock might have been right about the unknowable impact of their three-day journey into the past, she thought. But it was reassuring to see that some things never changed.

**Look for STAR TREK fiction from Pocket Books**

**Star Trek®**

*Enterprise: The First Adventure* • Vonda N. McIntyre
*Strangers From the Sky* • Margaret Wander Bonanno
*Final Frontier* • Diane Carey
*Spock's World* • Diane Duane
*The Lost Years* • J.M. Dillard
*Prime Directive* • Judith and Garfield Reeves-Stevens
*Probe* • Margaret Wander Bonanno
*Best Destiny* • Diane Carey
*Shadows on the Sun* • Michael Jan Friedman
*Sarek* • A.C. Crispin
*Federation* • Judith and Garfield Reeves-Stevens
*Vulcan's Forge* • Josepha Sherman & Susan Shwartz
*Mission to Horatius* • Mack Reynolds
*Vulcan's Heart* • Josepha Sherman & Susan Shwartz
*The Eugenics Wars: The Rise and Fall of Khan Noonien Singh, Books One* and *Two* • Greg Cox
*The Last Round-Up* • Christie Golden

Novelizations

*Star Trek: The Motion Picture* • Gene Roddenberry
*Star Trek II: The Wrath of Khan* • Vonda N. McIntyre
*Star Trek III: The Search for Spock* • Vonda N. McIntyre
*Star Trek IV: The Voyage Home* • Vonda N. McIntyre
*Star Trek V: The Final Frontier* • J.M. Dillard
*Star Trek VI: The Undiscovered Country* • J.M. Dillard
*Star Trek Generations* • J.M. Dillard
*Starfleet Academy* • Diane Carey

Star Trek books by William Shatner with Judith and Garfield Reeves-Stevens

*The Ashes of Eden*
*The Return*
*Avenger*
*Star Trek: Odyssey* (contains *The Ashes of Eden*, *The Return*, and *Avenger)*
*Spectre*
*Dark Victory*
*Preserver*

#1 • *Star Trek: The Motion Picture* • Gene Roddenberry
#2 • *The Entropy Effect* • Vonda N. McIntyre
#3 • *The Klingon Gambit* • Robert E. Vardeman
#4 • *The Covenant of the Crown* • Howard Weinstein
#5 • *The Prometheus Design* • Sondra Marshak & Myrna Culbreath
#6 • *The Abode of Life* • Lee Correy

#7 • *Star Trek II: The Wrath of Khan* • Vonda N. McIntyre
#8 • *Black Fire* • Sonni Cooper
#9 • *Triangle* • Sondra Marshak & Myrna Culbreath
#10 • *Web of the Romulans* • M.S. Murdock
#11 • *Yesterday's Son* • A.C. Crispin
#12 • *Mutiny on the Enterprise* • Robert E. Vardeman
#13 • *The Wounded Sky* • Diane Duane
#14 • *The Trellisane Confrontation* • David Dvorkin
#15 • *Corona* • Greg Bear
#16 • *The Final Reflection* • John M. Ford
#17 • *Star Trek III: The Search for Spock* • Vonda N. McIntyre
#18 • *My Enemy, My Ally* • Diane Duane
#19 • *The Tears of the Singers* • Melinda Snodgrass
#20 • *The Vulcan Academy Murders* • Jean Lorrah
#21 • *Uhura's Song* • Janet Kagan
#22 • *Shadow Lord* • Laurence Yep
#23 • *Ishmael* • Barbara Hambly
#24 • *Killing Time* • Della Van Hise
#25 • *Dwellers in the Crucible* • Margaret Wander Bonanno
#26 • *Pawns and Symbols* • Majliss Larson
#27 • *Mindshadow* • J.M. Dillard
#28 • *Crisis on Centaurus* • Brad Ferguson
#29 • *Dreadnought!* • Diane Carey
#30 • *Demons* • J.M. Dillard
#31 • *Battlestations!* • Diane Carey
#32 • *Chain of Attack* • Gene DeWeese
#33 • *Deep Domain* • Howard Weinstein
#34 • *Dreams of the Raven* • Carmen Carter
#35 • *The Romulan Way* • Diane Duane & Peter Morwood
#36 • *How Much for Just the Planet?* • John M. Ford
#37 • *Bloodthirst* • J.M. Dillard
#38 • *The IDIC Epidemic* • Jean Lorrah
#39 • *Time for Yesterday* • A.C. Crispin
#40 • *Timetrap* • David Dvorkin
#41 • *The Three-Minute Universe* • Barbara Paul
#42 • *Memory Prime* • Judith and Garfield Reeves-Stevens
#43 • *The Final Nexus* • Gene DeWeese
#44 • *Vulcan's Glory* • D.C. Fontana
#45 • *Double, Double* • Michael Jan Friedman
#46 • *The Cry of the Onlies* • Judy Klass
#47 • *The Kobayashi Maru* • Julia Ecklar
#48 • *Rules of Engagement* • Peter Morwood
#49 • *The Pandora Principle* • Carolyn Clowes
#50 • *Doctor's Orders* • Diane Duane

#51 • *Enemy Unseen* • V.E. Mitchell
#52 • *Home Is the Hunter* • Dana Kramer-Rolls
#53 • *Ghost-Walker* • Barbara Hambly
#54 • *A Flag Full of Stars* • Brad Ferguson
#55 • *Renegade* • Gene DeWeese
#56 • *Legacy* • Michael Jan Friedman
#57 • *The Rift* • Peter David
#58 • *Faces of Fire* • Michael Jan Friedman
#59 • *The Disinherited* • Peter David, Michael Jan Friedman, Robert Greenberger
#60 • *Ice Trap* • L.A. Graf
#61 • *Sanctuary* • John Vornholt
#62 • *Death Count* • L.A. Graf
#63 • *Shell Game* • Melissa Crandall
#64 • *The Starship Trap* • Mel Gilden
#65 • *Windows on a Lost World* • V.E. Mitchell
#66 • *From the Depths* • Victor Milan
#67 • *The Great Starship Race* • Diane Carey
#68 • *Firestorm* • L.A. Graf
#69 • *The Patrian Transgression* • Simon Hawke
#70 • *Traitor Winds* • L.A. Graf
#71 • *Crossroad* • Barbara Hambly
#72 • *The Better Man* • Howard Weinstein
#73 • *Recovery* • J.M. Dillard
#74 • *The Fearful Summons* • Denny Martin Flinn
#75 • *First Frontier* • Diane Carey & Dr. James I. Kirkland
#76 • *The Captain's Daughter* • Peter David
#77 • *Twilight's End* • Jerry Oltion
#78 • *The Rings of Tautee* • Dean Wesley Smith & Kristine Kathryn Rusch
#79 • *Invasion!* #1: *First Strike* • Diane Carey
#80 • *The Joy Machine* • James Gunn
#81 • *Mudd in Your Eye* • Jerry Oltion
#82 • *Mind Meld* • John Vornholt
#83 • *Heart of the Sun* • Pamela Sargent & George Zebrowski
#84 • *Assignment: Eternity* • Greg Cox
#85-87 • *My Brother's Keeper* • Michael Jan Friedman
  #85 • *Republic*
  #86 • *Constitution*
  #87 • *Enterprise*
#88 • *Across the Universe* • Pamela Sargent & George Zebrowski
#89-94 • *New Earth*
  #89 • *Wagon Train to the Stars* • Diane Carey
  #90 • *Belle Terre* • Dean Wesley Smith with Diane Carey
  #91 • *Rough Trails* • L.A. Graf
  #92 • *The Flaming Arrow* • Kathy and Jerry Oltion

#93 • *Thin Air* • Kristine Kathryn Rusch & Dean Wesley Smith
#94 • *Challenger* • Diane Carey
#95-96 • *Rihannsu* • Diane Duane
#95 • *Swordhunt*
#96 • *Honor Blade*
#97 • *In the Name of Honor* • Dayton Ward

**Star Trek®: The Original Series**

*The Janus Gate* • L.A. Graf
#1 • *Present Tense*
#2 • *Future Imperfect*
#3 • *Past Prologue*
*Errand of Vengeance* • Kevin Ryan
#1 • *The Edge of the Sword*

**Star Trek: The Next Generation®**

*Metamorphosis* • Jean Lorrah
*Vendetta* • Peter David
*Reunion* • Michael Jan Friedman
*Imzadi* • Peter David
*The Devil's Heart* • Carmen Carter
*Dark Mirror* • Diane Duane
*Q-Squared* • Peter David
*Crossover* • Michael Jan Friedman
*Kahless* • Michael Jan Friedman
*Ship of the Line* • Diane Carey
*The Best and the Brightest* • Susan Wright
*Planet X* • Michael Jan Friedman
*Imzadi II: Triangle* • Peter David
*I, Q* • John de Lancie & Peter David
*The Valiant* • Michael Jan Friedman
*The Genesis Wave, Books One, Two,* and *Three* • John Vornholt
*Immortal Coil* • Jeffrey Lang
*A Hard Rain* • Dean Wesley Smith
*The Battle of Betazed* • Charlotte Douglas & Susan Kearney

Novelizations

*Encounter at Farpoint* • David Gerrold
*Unification* • Jeri Taylor
*Relics* • Michael Jan Friedman
*Descent* • Diane Carey
*All Good Things...* • Michael Jan Friedman
*Star Trek: Klingon* • Dean Wesley Smith & Kristine Kathryn Rusch
*Star Trek Generations* • J.M. Dillard